Loose Ends

A MARY O'REILLY PARANORMAL MYSTERY

by

Terri Reid

Dedicated to my family, my friends, my readers and all those who hear a noise at night, blame it on the cat…but really know what made the sound.

Terri Reid

LOOSE ENDS – A MARY O'REILLY
PARANORMAL MYSTERY

by

Terri Reid

Copyright © 2010 by Terri Reid

Prologue

Galena, Illinois – 1980s

The candidate stood at the front of the ballroom a few feet behind the podium on a makeshift stage. He was young, tall and handsome. And behind the pretty-boy looks was a shrewd intelligence and quick wit that had won him respect, especially from his opponents. His lopsided grin, the one that could break hearts and win votes, was present as he had greeted his faithful volunteers and supporters.

The variety of the guests portrayed the eclectic spirit of the eighties. "Miami Vice" and "Material Girl" look-alikes mingled with Ralph Lauren and Armani aficionados. Wine, hard liquor and other, more discreetly served stimulants of choice, were sipped or inhaled in various venues throughout the mansion.

Trays of hors d'oeuvres were efficiently served and champagne was free flowing.

Soft lights emphasized subtle shades of blush and eye shadow, and flattered the complexions of aging society matrons. Clicking spiked heels crossing the marble floor from the doorway to the ballroom added a discordant beat to The Bangles' "Walk Like An Egyptian."

Red, white and blue crepe paper hung garishly against the oak paneled walls. Their patriotic theme was continued with bright banners hanging from the soaring ceiling of the ballroom.

The candidate surveyed his kingdom, smiled to himself in satisfaction and moved to the podium. He lifted his hands in welcome. The music was silenced, but the conversation of the crowd was deafening.

"We did it," he yelled above the clamoring of the crowd. "No, you did it! I would not be here tonight if not for you!"

As he expected, the crowd went wild. He had them convinced he was the only one capable of being their representative in the state senate. But that was only his first step; he had plans which included sitting behind the desk in the Oval Office.

"Of course, now comes the hard part," he yelled over the crowd, "saying something nice about my opponent to the media."

Once again the crowd responded with delight, chanting his name. "Ryerson, Ryerson, Ryerson!"

He waved at the crowd once more and stepped down from the stage. His eyes sought the corner of the room. His campaign manager, Hank Montague, stood at the back of the room, nodding his approval. The rest of the support staff – Jerry, Mike and Renee – stood next to Hank, raising their glasses in celebration. He smiled at them and then let his eyes rest for a moment longer on Renee.

Her honey-gold hair was wrapped up in a soft chignon tonight, but he remembered how it looked when it was loose, flowing over her body – their bodies. He gazed at the simple black dress she wore and imagined slowly peeling it off of her.

He stopped himself – letting his mind wander now could be dangerous. There were too many who were hoping for perfection, but looking for flaws.

He turned toward her once again and barely nodded. She understood; they had existed on shared secrets for several months now. He had to carefully consider his next steps, especially when it came to Renee. He couldn't afford a scandal – not now, when his political career had just taken off. Whatever he decided, he had to move quickly and make sure that any residual damage was minimized.

She caught his eye once more, lifted her glass in a subtle toast and grinned. The teasing in her eyes lasted until she stopped at the open French doors. She turned at the door and looked back over her shoulder, sending him another kind of look altogether. He felt the heat across the room. Coughing into his hand and nodding slightly, he signaled that he would be meeting her soon.

"So, where are you off to?" Jerry asked.

Renee smiled. "It's getting a little stuffy in here. Now that the announcement's been made, I'm going to catch a little air."

With her hand on the stone balustrade, she slipped off her high heels and stepped from the patio to the grass. The mild fall weather had encouraged late blooms and thick lawns. She inhaled the spicy scent of chrysanthemums as she wandered through the ornamental gardens. The full moon lit the way as she walked past arbors and fruit trees to the back of the gardens.

The incongruent scents of hardy mums, burning leaves, mesquite smoke and grilling steaks melded together to form a unique perfume that spoke of memories and possibilities.

She peeked over her shoulder once again before she slipped through a break in the tall hedge that surrounded the garden, and made her way cautiously across a small bridge. Following the path from the bridge, she found the wrought iron fence covered with ivy from years of growth. She lifted the well-oiled latch on the gate and slipped inside.

A beam of moonlight floated on the top of the water. Sitting at the edge of the pool, she slowly lowered her bare feet into the warm darkness. When he had first brought her out to the secluded heated pool, she thought it was the ultimate self-indulgence. But after spending some of their most intimate moments in the pool, she now thought of it as a definite necessity. She wiggled her toes – her movements causing the reflection to dance in soft waves against the other end of the pool. She giggled and splashed her feet flatly against the surface of the water. A small wave of moonlight splashed up against the opposite deck.

She lifted her glass for another sip of champagne and was surprised to find it empty. She licked the edge of the cup and sadly put it down on the mosaic tile.

The music from inside the house drifted out to her, slow and bluesy. Her body swayed to the sound. But even the blues couldn't dampen her spirits, for once in her life things were going to go her way.

She slowly rubbed her abdomen beneath her black silk sheath. *Yes, wonderful things are going to happen*, she thought.

He watched her slip through the gate. Perfect. Nice and private.

He moved swiftly and quietly down the path, making sure that he was not discovered.

Such a shame, she was a looker. But hey, you gotta clean up all the loose ends.

The gate opened noiselessly. His soft-soled shoes made no sound on the deck surrounding the pool.

She gasped in surprise when his hands came down on her shoulders. She tried to turn and look at him, but his fingers bit down on her shoulders, keeping her in place. Her angry cry quickly turned into a purr when he slowly massaged her back and her neck.

"I'm so glad you could meet me out here, I have such wonderful news for you," she said.

She felt a slight pinprick against her neck and tried to jump away, swatting at the invisible bug. But his hand held her firmly in place.

"Ow, damn mosquitoes!" she complained. "You really should spray some insecticide out here…"

She yawned softly and closed her eyes.

"I guess I'm feeling a little tired," she whispered, "too much champagne. I can't keep my eyes open."

Her body sank slowly down, she felt enveloped by the darkness. She looked up, saw the glitter of the moonlight above her and smiled.

Suddenly, her mind broke through the haze of the drug. She struggled against the strong arms holding her under the water. Her shouts surfaced as large bubbles of air, her thrashing arms and legs as soft waves against the sides of the pool. In a few moments the bubbles stopped, the waves became gentle ripples and Renee sank to the bottom of the pool.

"Oh, God, my baby!" was her last thought before she slipped away.

Chapter One

Present day

Moonlight stole through the living room windows of the small two-story home in the quiet town of Freeport, Illinois. Its light cast shadows around the tastefully decorated room, turning ordinary objects into spectral stalkers.

The wind ruffled the sheer curtains that swept over the polished wood floor. In the hall, an antique grandfather clock struck the hour of midnight. Clear tones echoed the twelve chimes throughout the quiet house.

Silence shrouded the home for a moment. Then a muffled noise came from behind the door that led from the basement stairs. *Thump. Thump. Thump.*

It moved closer. The polished ceramic doorknob rattled. *Thump. Thump. Thump.*

The door shook from the force of the blows. *Thump. Thump. Thump.*

Once again the lock and hinges held the door in place. *Thump. Thump. Thump.*

Finally, the wood around the brass lock splintered and the door crashed open.

He slowly shuffled from the doorway toward the staircase that led upstairs. Upstairs to the beautifully appointed bedroom. The bedroom where one woman slept. Alone and unprotected.

The wind moved through the curtains on the landing, midway up the stairs. The wind caught his scent and carried it forward – the sickly sweet scent of a decomposing body. He paused for a moment on the landing and then continued slowly up the stairs.

All of his movements were marked by a clear trail of blood. Streaks of blood mottled the floor, the Oriental rug and now, the top of the stairs.

The bedroom door at the end of the hall was slightly ajar. Thick white carpeting muffled his footsteps. He slowly pushed the door open and entered the room.

Moonlight spilled over the bed. Mary's long, light brown hair was spread across the pillowcase, a blanket covering half of her face. She was snoring lightly and her arm was stretched over her head.

He moved closer to the bed.

She wanted to hold her breath. The smell was almost too much to take. Instead, she concentrated on keeping her breath steady and rhythmic as if she were really asleep.

He stopped next to the bed and leaned forward. Hanging over her in the dark.

She heard the drops of blood hit the ivory 400-count down comforter. *Plunk. Plunk. Plunk.*

"Damn!"

She turned in her bed and looked up at him. He was dressed in gray, a Union soldier. His uniform was riddled with bullet holes and thick, red blood slowly seeped from each opening. But the blood dripping on her bed was not coming from those oozing apertures. No, the blood dripped from the stump where his head used to be. *Plunk. Plunk. Plunk.*

She watched as the blood pooled on the comforter.

"Crap, this is going to stain!"

She closed her eyes for a moment and then pushed herself up in her bed.

"Look, I've just had a really bad day and I can't deal with you tonight. Okay?"

He paused...and then straightened. After contemplating her response for a moment, he shrugged his shoulders, turned and slowly shuffled out of the room.

"And try to keep your blood off the new tiles in the kitchen," she called after him.

She put her elbows on her knees, laid her head in her hands and sighed. Was she ever going to get a good night's sleep?

Well, she might as well go and see what kind of mess he left downstairs.

She slipped out of her bed, examining the comforter for damage. Fortunately, when he had departed so had his blood.

"Bonus," she muttered.

Pulling on a short, silk robe, she tied it as she headed down the stairs. She watched him retreat through the broken door, then closed it and moved a chair in front of it in until she could replace the lock – this time, she decided, with a deadbolt.

"Deadbolt – good one," she chuckled.

Glancing around the room, she could see that other than a rumpled rug, he did surprisingly little damage.

"Not bad for a headless dead guy."

# # # #

The broadcaster's voice pierced the fog of sleep that encompassed Mary. She moaned and blindly reached out from her cocoon of blankets, trying to find the snooze button. Of course she couldn't reach it – she'd purposely placed the radio alarm far enough away from the bed so she had to get up to turn it off. She knew herself better than that.

Grumbling, she tossed the blankets off and stumbled across the room to her dresser. She flipped off the alarm and started to turn back to her inviting bed when she saw the yellow sports bra hanging as a reminder across the corner of the mirror.

Mary's eyes widened – *oh, yeah, the race!*

She groaned and opened her top drawer, grabbed the rest of her running gear and headed to the bathroom.

A few minutes later she was outside on her front porch, putting her half-asleep body through a series of stretches, while she inhaled slowly and deeply. She loved the scent of fall mornings. She turned toward the road and did her quad stretches, bending her right leg back and holding her right ankle with her hand.

She could tell someone in the neighborhood had used their fireplace last night, inhaling the faint aroma of burnt wood. Turning toward the porch, she slowly touched her toes. The dew was still heavy on the Marigolds and Mums in her front yard, the combination of spicy flower and damp soil filled her lungs. Somehow the morning air was fresher and more invigorating than any other time of the day. She glanced up to the thermometer on her porch, fifty-two degrees. Although the mid-October morning was chilly, she knew the day would warm up soon enough. Feeling stretched out, she jogged down the street toward the city park.

The streets were deserted and the morning sun was just barely peeking over the hill on the east side of town. She breathed in deeply. This was the nice thing about living in a small town: fresh air, quiet streets and interesting people.

Interesting people. She smiled to herself as she thought about the interesting person who was likely to be waiting for her at the park. Her mystery man. Her morning motivation. Her competitor.

At first, the meetings had been accidental. They both jogged in the park at the ungodly hour of five o'clock. They kept to the same path ‾ never speaking – but during the last lap an unspoken competition had developed. Both raced to the finish line, trying to outrun the other.

After a few weeks they waited for each other, still never speaking a word. Only a courtly nod of greeting and the race was on. Now, six months later, he was a regular part of her routine.

Mary jogged past the entrance of the park. This was another part of the small town that she loved. The park was located on one-hundred acres of grasslands, woods and limestone bluffs and would have made Norman Rockwell whistle with glee. Americana at its best: an old fashioned carousel, a band shell that hosted Sunday evening concerts in the summer, a baseball diamond for softball games and a nature trail for young lovers. That is, until the local police caught them.

Mary smiled as she turned onto the jogging path and headed toward the playground. Once she crested the hill she could see the playground and him – stretching.

Oh wow, she thought, *he does that really well*.

She took in his usual garb – a pair of cut-off sweats and a muscle tee.

I wonder if he ever considered Spandex? she mused, as she jogged closer. Probably wouldn't be too polite to suggest it.

Besides, she actually liked him better because he wasn't into designer athletic gear. His clothes seemed to match him: down to earth, hard-working, honest. His brown hair was slightly shaggy and he never shaved before he ran.

He's stubborn, demanding and used to having his own way, Mary silently decided. Pretty good for never having spoken to the guy.

She grinned.

She passed the teeter-totters and jogged up to the swing sets where he waited.

He smiled and nodded.

Mary nodded in response.

They took their places and ran.

The run was great – fast and hard. It cleared the cobwebs out of her mind, but her nocturnal visitor had taken its toll. Her competitor was pulling out in front. She hated to lose – no, she *really* hated to lose. Quickly, she assessed the situation. In a moment they would be reaching the fork in the road. The high path was smoother, but it was uphill. The lower path gave you downhill momentum, but you also had to go through the band shell obstacle course. If she could hurdle those three park benches, she would more than make up for his speed. Deciding, she took the downhill path on the left and ran toward the white band shell. Gauging the height of the first bench, she gathered herself and jumped.

She easily cleared it and ran the few yards to the next, sailing over with no trouble. Heading for the third, she glanced over her shoulder. She could see that he had nearly caught up with her. Pushing harder, she leapt over the last bench, came down a little unsteady, caught herself and sprinted to the finish line.

She touched the tall chain-link fence around the merry-go-round only moments before he did.

Breathing heavily, she bent over and placed her hands on her knees. Mary wiped the sweat from her forehead and turned to him. He was as winded as she, his t-shirt soaked with perspiration, his hands on his knees. He caught her glance, grinned, and winked in approval.

She returned the grin, straightened and started the slow jog back to her house without looking back.

It was going to be a good day.

Chapter Two

The tall brownstone office building sat in the midst of a decaying downtown. It seemed people preferred to shop in the strip malls or the "Marts" that were located where the urban sprawl had guided them, rather than in the quaint storefronts of yesteryear.

Mary pulled her car into the diagonal parking spot in front of her office and stepped out. She gazed up and down the nearly deserted street, enjoying the fact that the folks who usually wandered down Main Street were there for a purpose, rather than spoiled teenagers with time to kill. She also liked the atmosphere of the area and could feel the past generations of townsfolk who had walked down the street, looking for the new shoes for Suzie and the baseball mitt for Tommy.

Her gift allowed her to catch a glimpse of the past. Shadows of young boys dressed in dungarees and cotton shirts, pressing their noses against the storefront window, coveting the new Red Flyer wagon or Keds tennis shoes. Teenage couples making doe-eyes over a shared ice cream soda. A uniformed soldier hugging his girl goodbye before the bus carried him away to war.

Sometimes she wondered about the rest of their stories. Unfortunately, she only got part of the picture, unless she was able to research and follow the story through. These shadows walked in and out of her life like commercials during primetime. She had a glimpse of their lives, but not the whole story.

She unlocked the door to her office and switched on the lights. The answering machine light was blinking. That was always a good sign, unless it was a desperate telemarketer.

Just before she clicked the messages button her phone rang.

"O'Reilly Investigations, Mary speaking," she said.

"He's dead!" the voice on the other end of the phone cried. "I came in this morning and tried everything – he's just dead."

Mary smiled, recognizing the voice of her two-doors-down neighbor, Rosie Pettigrew, a highly successful real estate broker.

"Calm down, Rosie," she said, "I'm sure we can revive Mel."

Mary pictured Rosie waving a lace handkerchief at her face while she clutched the phone in her other hand. Rosie was in her early sixties, but had the appearance and energy of a woman much younger. She was always outfitted as if she were expecting to take tea at the White House.

She had buried four husbands, raised five children and gone through three careers. She was extremely confident and looked to each new challenge as an adventure, except for one area of her life – computers.

She had named her computer Mel because – as she explained to Mary – anything that took this much time out a woman's life, caused as many headaches and, on occasion, gave a woman pleasure beyond belief, had to be a man.

"No, Mary, I'm sure he's dead this time," Rosie cried. "Can you come over and have a look?"

Mary glanced at the blinking light on her answering machine and shook her head.

"Sorry, Rosie, I might actually have a client. Let me give you a couple of over-the-phone pointers and we'll see if we can get Mel back to his old sexy self."

Rosie sighed audibly. "Fine, we can try. But I tell you, Mary, he's dead for sure this time."

"Okay, first click on the button on the monitor – anything?"

Mary heard the click and waited.

"No, nothing," Rosie said. "That little green light isn't even coming on."

"Okay," Mary said, "now try turning the computer on again. Do you hear any sounds?"

"No, nothing at all," Rosie responded after a moment.

"Okay – check the power strip. Is the switch in the 'On' position?"

"Yes, the switch is on – but the red light on the power switch isn't even lit up!" Rosie groaned with frustration.

Mary smiled.

"Okay, Rosie, I want you to unplug the power switch and plug your lamp into that socket."

"What?"

"Just trust me on this one," Mary replied.

"This is what I get for asking a ghostbuster for help," Mary could hear Rosie muttering. "How the hell is plugging in a lamp going to fix my computer?"

Mary grinned and sat back in her chair.

"Oh no!" she heard Rosie cry out. "Now my lamp isn't working!"

Mary could hear Rosie pick up the phone.

"Did you hear that?" Rosie cried. "Now my lamp isn't working either! What's going on?"

"Rosie, I want you to take a deep breath," Mary said.

She could hear Rosie forcing herself to calm and breathe slowly.

"Now, go to your switchbox and fix the blown fuse."

"My fuse?" Rosie asked, confused for a moment.

Then, a soft giggle. "Well, damn, of course, my fuse – how silly. Thanks, Mary."

"No problem, Rosie," Mary replied. "Have a great day."

Mary hung up the phone with a smile on her face. "Gotta love small towns."

The blinking light on her answering machine now demanded its turn. She sat on the edge of the desk, grabbed a memo pad and pen and pressed the button.

"Hello, Miss…er…O'Reilly… Um, this is…this is Susan Ryerson. I would like you to call me as soon as possible. My cell number is 815-555-8989. Please call me back today – during the day, or tomorrow, anytime. And please keep this call strictly confidential. Thank you."

Well, this ought to be interesting, Mary thought, *the State Senator's wife calling me for help. Perhaps the skeletons in his closet aren't staying nice and quiet for him.*

She picked up the phone and dialed the number. It rang once and the voice that left the message anxiously answered.

"Hello, this is Mary O'Reilly, you left a message?"

"Yes, yes," Susan Ryerson replied hurriedly. "Can we meet?"

"Sure, when and where?"

Susan named a small cafe in a nearby town and explained that she could be there in a few minutes.

"Okay, it'll take me about an hour before I can meet you," Mary answered. "Do you want to give me any information before we meet?"

"No, no," she whispered. "I'll tell you all about it when I see you."

Mary hung up the phone and tapped the pencil thoughtfully against her chin. Well, this probably would be a job that actually paid. That would be a nice change.

She slipped around the desk, into the chair, clicked on her computer and waited for it to boot up. Once the computer was online, she retrieved her e-mail, deleted all the obvious spam and saved the messages she wanted to read. Except for one. She hesitated for a moment, rereading the sender information – Hamilton County Genealogical Society. Taking a deep breath, she clicked on the message. It opened on the screen.

"The information you requested on Lt. Earl Belvidere is as follows:

Birth Certificate – available

Record of Military Service – available

Notice of Death – available

Place of Burial – unavailable

Note: Only relatives of the deceased may view these records. If you are a relative, submit your name, mailing information and relationship to the deceased in a self-addressed stamped envelope. Please include $3.00 for each record you wish to have copied."

The remainder of the message listed the address of the society.

Mary pulled out a piece of stationary and started to write – after all, he was living in her basement, surely that warranted some kind of legal relationship.

She began the letter.

To whom it may concern,

My dear departed great, great uncle Earl Belvidere…

A few minutes later with the completed letter in hand, she packed up her briefcase with a new yellow legal pad, a working pen and her cell phone. She glanced in the mirror, quickly applied some lipstick and headed out the door.

As she walked to the car, she was greeted by her next door neighbor, Stanley Wagner, who was seated on his favorite bench. Stanley had the appearance of a seventy year old, the mind of a thirty year old and the sense of humor of a teenager. He wore his round spectacles low on his nose and his eyebrows high on his forehead.

Stanley was the fifth generation owner of Wagner's Office Supplies, affectionately referred to as Stanley's by everyone in town. His store carried everything from bottles of ink for replenishing stamp pads to rubber thimbles for flipping through piles of paper. He carried every weight of stationery you could imagine and envelopes to match. He knew his customers by name, the kind of stationery and pens they favored, the width and length of tapes their office machines needed and the names of all of their spouses and children. But rather than reward this unique kind of old-fashioned service, most of Stanley's customers had taken their business to the new office supply superstore that had just been built on the south side of town.

In spite of that, Stanley's still opened every morning at seven. And even though the sixth generation of Wagners now ran the store, Stanley was outside every morning greeting the day.

"Morning, Mary," Stanley said, looking up from the newspaper.

"Morning, Stanley," she replied moving toward the car. "What's the good news?"

"The new police chief has got some more ideas about our parking spaces in the downtown area," Stanley answered, his eyes twinkling with glee.

Although Mary had never met the new police chief, she could just picture him: size forty-eight waist with a six-inch muffin-top, receding hairline, large red nose, small squinty eyes and an intelligence quotient that topped at double digits.

"So, what is Barney Fife up to now?" she asked.

Stanley chuckled. "Well, he's thinking that parking meters would work well to bring more income to the city."

Mary rolled her eyes.

"Has he even visited downtown on a weekday?"

She looked down the nearly vacant street.

"Who does he think is going to be feeding all of the meters?"

"Well," Stanley said thoughtfully, "there'd be me and you and Rosie."

Mary chuckled. "You're right Stanley – that'd be about it."

She turned, shaking her head.

"I've got to go – I've got an appointment. But if you notice Barney Fife hanging around here trying to plant some parking meters, you can tell him where I think he ought to stuff…"

Stanley lifted his hand to stop her.

"I'd best just refer him to you, if I don't want to spend some time in the hoosegow," he chuckled.

Mary laughed. "Yes, I suppose that would be best."

Chapter Three

Mary pressed the accelerator pedal of her black 1965 MGB Roadster and shifted into fifth as she left the town of Stockton behind her. She loved the drive from Freeport to the small town of Galena. It was as if a bit of New England had been transplanted into the Midwest, complete with rolling hills and limestone bluffs. The highway twisted and turned through farmland and small towns, providing breathtaking vistas from the tops of the closest thing Illinois could claim as a mountain.

Red, gold and orange foliage seem to cover every spot that wasn't a road or a building. The air blowing through the vents smelled of leaves burning and crisp air. This was Mary's favorite time of year.

She drove through Tapley Woods, a lovely forested area on the outskirts of Galena, and then shifted down to fourth gear as she entered the city limits. Originally, Galena had been a mining town, but was now a trendy vacation spot for Chicagoans who wanted a retreat in the country. The streets were narrow, red brick-lined and hilly. The historic brick stores were now upscale and unique.

"Come on," Mary growled, as she passed yet another car whose driver had decided to take a parking spot and a half at the crowded curb, "who taught you how to parallel park?"

Once she found a parking spot a block from the small café, she grabbed her briefcase, locked her car and casually strolled down the street. The large showcase shop windows gave her ample opportunity to study herself coming and, if the angle was right, going. She hated to admit it, but she was slightly intimidated by women like Susan Ryerson. Perfect political partner. Sophisticated and highly educated. Born with a silver spoon in her mouth.

Glancing at herself in one of the store windows, she tucked a loose strand of hair back in place and checked her lipstick. She was glad she had decided on wool tailored slacks, silk blouse and tweed jacket that morning.

She smiled. *Not only am I making a fashion statement, I'm not freezing my butt off.*

The café was quaint and inviting, with a small blazing fireplace in one corner, solid wooden tables and chairs, and vintage tin signs on the walls. She inhaled the warm flavors that greeted her as she entered: freshly roasted coffee, cinnamon pastries and – she paused for a moment – pumpkin. A quick glance to the Specials board advertising Pumpkin Bisque confirmed her conclusion.

Even if she hadn't seen Susan on television a number of times, she would have been able to pick her new client out from the primarily blue jean clad clientele. Mary took a moment to study her. She had chosen a table in the far corner of the café, where she assumed they would have some privacy.

Susan was impeccably dressed in a wool boucle suit with black pumps. Her silver-blonde hair was cut in a sleek cap over her head. She looked like the picture of cool sophistication, something out of a magazine.

Then Mary looked at Susan's hands sliding up and down over the outside of her oversized latte mug. She was not as calm as she tried to project. *Not as cool and calm as she looks,* Mary thought with a smile. *Why does that make me feel better?*

She stopped at the bar and ordered an herb tea before strolling over and introducing herself to her next client.

"Hi," she said, extending her hand as she slipped into the chair across from Susan, "I'm Mary O'Reilly. It's nice to meet you."

Susan Ryerson shook the offered hand and pasted a strained smile on her face.

"Susan Ryerson. Thank you for coming."

Mary paused for a moment as her tea was delivered to the table and then pulled the yellow legal pad out of her briefcase.

"Do you mind if I take notes?" she asked the senator's wife.

Susan shook her head. "No, not at all. I would prefer if I don't have to repeat anything."

Mary nodded and tapped her pen on her hand. "Why don't you begin by telling me why you called me today?"

Susan shook her head. "Before I do that, can you tell me a little bit about your company and what it is you do?"

Mary smiled and nodded.

"My background is in criminal justice. Police work is part of my DNA. My grandfather, my dad, my older brothers and I were all Chicago cops. It was the only career I ever considered.

"I went to University of Illinois, got a degree and started as a rookie on the force. I did pretty well. Moved up quickly. I was in line to become a detective. I figure if I had put in another six months, I would have been promoted."

"What happened?"

Mary sighed and unconsciously rubbed her hand just below her left shoulder. "A stake-out gone bad," she said, shrugging. "I ended up in the middle of a gang war. Not a place you want to be."

"You were shot?" Susan asked, stunned.

"Not only shot, I died," Mary replied.

Susan's eyes widened.

"Yeah, I did that whole 'walk to the light' thing," Mary said flippantly. Then she took a deep breath and met Susan's eyes, her face now somber.

"I still remember looking down on my body. My whole family was there in the hospital room," she said softly. "I saw my mother sobbing, and my dad, he just looked so old all of the sudden. I knew that I – my death – had caused it.

"Then I got a choice," she continued. "I heard a voice – called me by name. He gave me a choice to go back, if I wanted. But told me if I chose to return, things wouldn't quite be the same."

She smiled and shook her head.

"I figured, you know, that I'd walk with a limp or something. Oh, no, nothing as simple as that. When I came back I was able to see people who had died. People who hadn't gone to the light, who needed to resolve some issues in order to get there. So here I am – doing investigations to help move people on."

"So, do many people have ghosts that they need you to help move on?" Susan asked.

Mary laughed, thinking of her night-time visitor. "No, most of my customers are the ghosts themselves. It makes giving out references a bitch, but, hey, it's a living."

Mary leaned back in her chair. "So, now that you know my story, why don't you tell me yours?"

Susan took a deep breath, leaned forward in her chair and whispered, "First, I need to be assured that everything I say is held in the strictest confidence."

"Of course."

Susan studied Mary's eyes for a moment, then continued, "I believe my husband and I are being haunted. And I believe the ghost is a young woman who died at our home many years ago."

Mary sipped her tea. After a moment she asked, "Why would someone, this young woman, haunt you?"

Susan's eyes glanced away for a moment and then met Mary's straight on.

"Because she might not have just died as we assumed. I think she might have been murdered."

Chapter Four

That evening Mary found herself once again navigating the winding roads that twisted through the northwest landscape of Illinois. It was tricky driving on them during the day, but on a cold, drizzly fall evening, the roads could be considered close to treacherous. Not only did Mary have to worry about meeting white-tailed deer on the road, she also had to keep her temper when non-local drivers sped past her like they were on an interstate, rather than a two-lane highway.

"If you crash and end up a ghost, don't come to me begging for help," she muttered as a sporty Mercedes whizzed past her at a tricky overpass. Mary tightened her grip on the steering wheel and shook her head, "Idiots!"

She entered the Tapley Woods Conservation Area and slowed down. If there was any place on this road for a run-in with a white-tail, this would be it. A movement and a glimmer of white in the woods drew her attention, but disappeared before she could get a good look at it.

Exiting Tapley Woods, she turned right on a road leading to a ridge overlooking the town of Galena. The homes in this area were an eclectic combination of estates and week-end hunting retreats. She found the address Susan Ryerson had given her and pulled into the drive. This was no week-end hunting retreat. The stately mansion stood about a half mile back from the road and looked imposing sitting on the slight rise before her.

She put the car into first gear and continued slowly up the drive, glancing carefully at the tall trees that stood on either side. The vegetation made it nearly impossible for her to see the grounds beyond the drive. But the familiar chill running down her spine told her the house was indeed hiding a secret.

She parked in the circular drive and climbed the marble steps to the oversized oak door. She only waited a few moments after pressing the doorbell before she could hear the sharp clicking of high heels against ceramic tile. Susan opened the door and invited Mary inside.

"I'm grateful that you could come tonight," Susan said. "Joseph, the senator, is in Chicago and I really didn't want him to be here when you came."

"Have you talked to him about the ghost?" Mary asked.

Susan shook her head. "No. But I've seen him looking at the same area I've seen her. Because he doesn't speak about it, I thought perhaps it was too painful."

"Have you considered that this is something he would rather not have investigated?" she asked.

Susan's eyes widened for a moment. "Why wouldn't he...?" she paused. "Are you saying that you think my husband might have been involved with her murder?"

31

Mary shrugged.

"I'm not drawing any assumptions yet – I haven't even seen the ghost. But if I find out that there was a murder and he was involved, I can't leave it there. I'll have to investigate," she replied firmly.

"Is that some kind of private investigator's rule?" Susan asked.

Mary shook her head.

"No, it's my rule. I'm all about getting these ghosts to the other side. And they won't go until things are settled.

"So, do you want me to continue?" Mary asked.

Susan paused a moment and linked her hands together at her waist. "Well, I guess it comes down to trust," she said, almost to herself. She looked up and nodded.

"Yes, I trust Joseph. I don't think he had anything to do with her murder," she said firmly. "Yes, I want you to continue."

Mary hoped Susan's trust was well placed.

"Great, then let's get going," she said. "Where do you see the ghost?"

Susan led Mary across the hall and opened a large door.

"This is the ballroom," she said, as they entered the room. "The kids actually used it for roller skating when they were young. Now, it mostly sits empty."

She walked over to a grouping of switches and flicked on a few, casting the room into dim light.

The room was about the size of the gymnasium at the local high school.

"Wow," Mary said, "nice."

The room had soaring ceilings with crystal chandeliers, a parquet wood floor, a wall of leaded glass windows and French doors that led to a stone-covered terrace.

In one corner sat a gleaming black grand piano that looked like it was well used. There were chairs pushed back against the wall and a rolled up rug against another.

"The first time I saw her, I was searching for some sheet music," Susan said, walking across the room to the grand piano. "I keep music in the bench."

They reached the piano and Susan pointed across the room near the terrace doors.

"She appeared there," she said. "Then she walked out through the French doors."

Mary nodded and reached into her pocket for her penlight.

"Are you prepared to follow her tonight?" she asked.

Susan looked startled for a moment. "Do you need me?" she asked.

Mary hid a smile. She had almost forgotten that the general population would rather not have to know that ghosts exist, much less follow them around.

"If you want to come, I'd welcome your input," Mary said, "but you have to decide what makes you feel comfortable."

Susan bit her lower lip nervously.

"Why don't we wait and see what happens," she suggested.

Mary nodded, slipped her penlight back into her pocket and pulled a notebook out of her purse. "Why don't I ask you a couple of questions to help me in my research," she said.

Susan sat on the bench and Mary leaned against the piano, her pen posed on the paper.

"About what time of day did you see her?" she asked.

"It was about eight-thirty at night," Susan replied.

Mary watched Susan's eyes flick nervously across the room.

"And the other times, when you came back at the same time, did she reappear?"

Susan's startled eyes flew back to Mary. "How do, how did...?" she stammered.

"You're a curious and intelligent woman," Mary shrugged. "Of course you'd come back here to make sure it wasn't your imagination or a passing car light reflected in the windows. So, how many times?"

Susan shrugged. "I've seen her four additional times since the first night," she admitted, "always at the same time, always in the same place."

Mary nodded and noted it. She watched Susan fidget and wondered what else the woman was not telling her. She only had a few minutes before the ghost was scheduled to appear, so she'd have to trust her gut.

"Can I have a copy of the information you've found on the woman who died?" she asked in a matter-of-fact voice.

Once again, Susan looked flustered, and then shook her head.

"You are very good at this, aren't you?"

Mary smiled. "I'm the best."

Susan looked up and her eyes caught across the room. Mary followed her gaze. In the far corner, a soft haze appeared close to the French doors. The haze began to take shape and in a moment they were staring at a dark-haired young woman, dressed in a short dress.

"I'll have the files waiting for you, when you get back," Susan whispered, her voice shaky.

Mary nodded, her attention on the movements of the ghost across the room. She watched as the ghost looked around the room and smiled, motioning with her eyes and with subtle movements to someone unseen. Then, with a last secretive smile, she slid out of the room through the French doors.

Mary called back to Susan as she jogged across the room, "I'll try to find out what she wants."

Mary pushed open the French doors, scanning the terrace with her flashlight. At the far corner, she saw the ghost slowly gliding down the stairs toward the garden. Mary followed.

The evening sky was dark – clouds covered the nearly full moon and the stars – but thankfully the rain had stopped. Mary pulled her jacket tighter and followed the translucent glow across the lawn, trying to avoid slipping on the wet leaves that carpeted the grass. Beyond the manicured lawn, the informal garden was overgrown with trees and vegetation. Mary pushed through the wet, dead limbs to find the path that the ghost slid through effortlessly.

"Someone needs to fire the gardener," Mary muttered, when a particularly lethal-looking branch just missed her face. "Or shoot him."

Once through the barrier of the garden, Mary felt the landscape begin to slope downward. The grass was knee-high, but she had a clearer view of the ghost.

She stumbled forward, her foot catching on a hidden root, and ended up on her hands and knees on the muddy path. "Crap!" Looking up quickly to be sure she didn't lose the direction of the ghost, she was rewarded with a splash of cold water that dripped onto her head, down her forehead and into her eyes. Wiping her eyes with her sleeve, she scurried to her feet and half jogged down the trail to catch up. She saw her about fifteen feet further up the path when the ghost drifted behind a tall dense wall of privet hedges and disappeared from view.

"Oh, no, you don't," Mary panted and broke into a run. She pushed through the hedge and found herself in an old maze. The walls reached above her head and a narrow aisle of about three feet separated them. Her flashlight beam bounced off the ragged edges of the brush and created eerie shadow figures that seemed to be reaching out skeletal hands, ready to pull her into their grasp. She paused and took a deep breath.

"Get a grip, O'Reilly. You chase ghosts for a living for heaven's sakes," she muttered and continued her jog up the aisle.

She flashed her light ahead and was greeted with three path choices. None looked particularly welcoming.

"Choose the right," she sang softly, repeating the words from a childhood Sunday school song. But just as she moved toward the right, the glimpse of a white, translucent leg disappearing at the end of the one on the left had Mary jogging down that narrow passageway. "Sure hope it's the same ghost."

She turned at the end of the row and was greeted by a dead end. "I know I saw her come this way."

Mary turned and flashed her light around the small enclosure, carefully studying the growth in front of her. A shape incongruent with nature caught her attention and she reached forward through the hedge and clasped cold metal. She pushed the brush aside and found a wrought iron fence. Jiggling the latch several times to loosen the rusted mechanism, she forced it open and strained against the plant covered gate. Finally it started to move and Mary put her weight against it. The gate inched slowly forward and Mary squeezed through.

"Crap, this rust is going to stain," she muttered as the gate caught at her clothing.

But her concern about the damage to her wardrobe was instantly erased when she slipped past the gate and stepped into a different world.

"Whoa."

The temperature was suddenly warm. *Downright balmy, like summer,* she thought. *I have now entered "The Twilight Zone."*

The garden was manicured and little lights were placed strategically along the paved walkway. She could hear water flowing ahead, beyond a privacy wall. She followed the path and skirted the wall.

The water was turquoise blue, reflecting the color of the swimming pool. Patio furniture surrounded the pool, waiting for a party. Moving forward she saw the ghost sitting on the edge of the pool, her feet slapping against the surface of the water. She heard her laugh – an echo of a laugh from a long time ago.

Mary moved forward to see if the ghost would speak with her, but before she could move, the story started to unfold before her eyes. The ghost laughed and leaned back, her voice was too low for Mary to hear. But she could see her whispering, an intimate conversation like she was talking to a lover. The ghost slid into the water, floating for a moment.

That's strange, Mary thought, *she's not dressed for swimming.*

Slowly the translucent woman drifted under the water, her eyes open, her smile dreamy. Mary watched, transfixed, as she drifted in the pool of blue.

Then her eyes widened and her smile turned to fear. Bubbles rushed to the surface of the pool as the ghost struggled against the unseen force that held her under.

Mary moved to help, but stopped, remembering she was seeing a vision of the past. Finally, after a few of the longest minutes in Mary's life, the bubbles stopped and the body drifted to the bottom of the pool.

Instantly, the scene changed. Mary was staring at an abandoned pool, cracks in the sides, weeds growing up from the dirt collected on the bottom.

Gone was the furniture, patio lights and neatly manicured gardens. In their place was darkness, neglect and the frigid sensation of death. A cold spot. Mary shivered before the cold wind reminded her she was back in the present.

She flashed her light beam around the area and then down into the pool where the body had drifted moments before. Only cracked concrete was visible.

Mary took a deep shuddering breath. This had not been an accidental drowning. Someone had indeed murdered this woman.

She turned and found herself face to face with the phantom. Wet hair was plastered against her ice-blue face. Her clothing dripped with water, her eyes intense. Mary gasped and stepped back, her heart thudding against her chest.

She took a quick calming breath. "How, how can I help you?"

Mary could feel the grief emanating from the ghost in front of her. Tears filled the ghost's eyes. Instinctively, Mary reached out – only to find her hand moving through the ethereal body.

"Let me help you," she repeated.

The ghost shook her head slowly. "Why did he kill me? Why did he kill my baby?" she whispered and faded into the dark night.

A formal tea was laid out in the parlor when Mary returned. Susan Ryerson sat stiffly on the edge of a small loveseat, her hands clasped in her lap. Although her body language screamed that she was tense, her smile was welcoming and warm.

A perfect political wife, Mary thought as she walked across the room and sat directly across from Susan. *But would she kill for her husband?*

"Were you able to follow her?" Susan asked, biting her lower lip.

Mary nodded, helped herself to a cup of tea and sipped slowly. She watched Susan over the rim of her cup. Her granddad had taught her that sometimes you learn more by keeping quiet than by questioning a suspect. As far as she was concerned, Susan Ryerson was still on the list.

Susan twisted her hands in her lap.

"Did she say anything?" she asked.

Mary took her time replacing her cup in the saucer and then met Susan's eyes. She needed to do some investigation before she mentioned everything she had learned from the ghost – especially the part about the baby.

"She was murdered." she stated baldly. "Someone held her under the water until she drowned."

Susan tried to cover her gasp and schooled her features into calm. But when she reached for her own cup of tea, her hand was shaking too much to lift the cup. Mary reached across the small table and placed her hand over Susan's. Susan lifted her head and looked into Mary's eyes.

"Do you, does she know…?" Susan stumbled.

"She doesn't know who killed her and neither do I," Mary answered. "And I'm not going to draw any conclusions until I get more information."

Susan reached for a large manila envelope and handed it to Mary.

"I pulled the local newspaper archives about her death. At the time everyone thought it was an accidental drowning," she said. "I never questioned it, until…"

"Until you saw the ghost for yourself?" Mary added.

Susan nodded.

"I also pulled her old personnel record from my husband's campaign files," she said. "She was his assistant."

Mary nodded, opened the file and glanced through the information.

"Renee Peterson," she said, reading from the employment application. "She was born in 1960 – so she would have been about twenty-four years old when she died."

Susan nodded.

"We all thought it was a shame that such a bright young girl had died," Susan said.

Mary watched her start to say something else and then stop.

"Did you know her very well?" Mary asked.

Susan shook her head.

"No. Although I was an active campaign wife, I was also a mother of small children," she explained. "So my husband spent most of the time on the campaign – I made whatever trips I could."

"And, as his assistant, did she travel with him?"

Susan took a deep breath.

"Are you asking me if my husband was involved in an affair with her?" she asked.

Mary nodded. "Yes, I am."

Susan pressed her lips into a firm line.

"Yes, I believe he was having an affair with her," she said, "and quite frankly, I think he was seriously considering leaving me for her. Of course, if you repeat that to anyone, I'll deny it."

Mary nodded.

"Our marriage was not going well in those days," she admitted. "I was deeply involved with our children, trying to be mother and father. Joseph was involved in his career. We didn't always see eye to eye on things."

"So, had he mentioned divorce to you?"

42

"No," she said, shaking her head. "But I could tell there was something going on. And then when they found her body, he was completely devastated. I could tell how deeply he must have loved her."

"Didn't that make you angry?"

Susan sighed.

"I was hurt, betrayed, and yes, angry. But I also knew my place had to be at Joseph's side. It was right after he had won the senate seat," she explained. "We both had to put on appropriate faces for the public."

She picked up her cup and stopped before she sipped.

"I really hated it," she said, placing her cup down with enough force that the saucer rattled on the table. "Hated smiling when inside I was dying. I hated the man that stood next to me. I hated that he thought he could replace me for a younger model."

"So, what happened? Why are you still with him?"

"Renee's death changed Joseph," she said. "He started taking the time to be with the children and me. He started to turn back into the man I fell in love with. It took a long time, but we were both able to put some things behind us and move on."

Mary nodded. *Was the murder of a young woman one of those things?* she wondered.

"I'll need a list of all the people who were at your house that night, including the names of any staff," she said.

43

"It's already in the folder." Susan almost smiled at Mary's look of surprise. "I was a devoted fan of detective novels; I understand that you need a list of possible suspects."

"That's helpful, thanks," Mary said and slipped the envelope under her arm. "I'll begin working on this right away and give you regular reports."

Susan stood. "And if you should find…"

"If I find that your husband is involved with the murder, I'll notify the police," Mary said, "and then I'll call you."

Susan nodded. "He's not, you know…he's not involved. I would have known."

Mary thought about all of the other women who had said that to her during her time on the police force. She shook Susan's hand and smiled.

"I can see myself out."

Chapter Five

Mary decided to forgo her early morning run and headed to the office first thing the next morning. She liked driving through the town when most of its occupants were still sleeping. The streetlights shone dimly in the hazy morning sky. Paper carriers were still walking down the oak-lined streets, tossing the Freeport Republic onto the front steps of residences. A couple of early morning runners jogged down one of the side streets. And one slightly disgruntled terry-robed gentleman stood on his lawn, urging his little dog to finish its business and get back into the house. The dog, on the other hand, seemed quite content to enjoy its early morning constitution.

With Harry Connick, Jr. crooning at her from her radio, Mary was in a fairly mellow mood when she pulled her car up in front of her office. She grabbed her purse, briefcase and a bag containing her lunch and got out of the car.

She stepped up on the curb and recoiled quickly, peripherally seeing a figure lurking behind the light pole out of the corner of her eye. "Crap," she reminded herself, "those damn scarecrows."

The plywood scarecrow attached to the light pole, one of many that decorated the downtown in the fall, had done a darn good job of scaring her once again. When would she ever remember they were there?

She unlocked her door, flipped on the light and put her bags on her desk. The light on her answering machine was not blinking, so she knew there were no urgent matters to attend to and she could concentrate on the Ryerson case.

About an hour later she had confirmed her initial feelings: there would be no easy Internet search in her investigation into the murder of Renee Peterson. She stretched her blue jeans clad legs and glanced over at the vintage schoolhouse clock on the wall – it was nearly seven. She was sure someone would be at the offices of the Freeport Republic. Although Susan Ryerson had copied the article, Mary wanted to see if there was any more information about the drowning victim.

She walked the two blocks over to the newspaper office and tried the front door. Locked. Mary shrugged and went around the back to the loading dock. She greeted the crew from the circulation department as she hoisted herself up on the dock.

"Hi guys, anyone inside yet?"

Dutch, the forty-year veteran of the crew, smiled and nodded toward the door. "Yeah, I already heard Wiley screaming about something this morning."

"Hmmm, well, maybe I ought to wait until later," Mary mused. "I needed to ask him a favor."

"Hey, one look at you and he'll forget what he was grumbling about," Dutch said with a wink.

Mary grinned. "So, when are you going to run away with me?"

"Soon as the wife says I can go," he replied.

Mary sighed loudly. "Well, she knows she's got a good thing. I don't see her letting you go anytime soon."

"You're young, you'll get over it."

Mary laughed.

"So, you think I'm fickle. That hurts, Dutch, that really hurts."

She pushed through the "Employees Only" door into the newspaper.

The smell of ink and the deep rumbling of machinery radiated from the labyrinth of large presses and rollers, inhabiting the press room. The bare light bulb suspended from the ceiling cast shadows over the hulking monsters as huge rolls of paper were consumed, stamped, cut and collated into newsprint, advertising and special sections.

She circumvented the massive printing presses to reach the door leading into the newsroom. She pushed it open and entered yet another dimly lit room. Because the Republic was a morning paper, most of the staff worked late into the evening to offer the residents the latest breaking news. So at seven-fifteen a.m. the newsroom was usually deserted.

Row upon row of ancient metal desks with high tech computers sat empty, an occasional glow from a screen saver illuminating the area around it. She didn't look too closely at the dark corners in the room. She understood more than most, that dedicated reporters never give up on a good story.

Across the room, the light from the editor's office glimmered in the corner. Glass walls allowed Jerry Wiley, editor-in-chief, to keep an eye on his employees, but they also offered those outside the office a bird's eye view of everything Jerry did.

Mary took a moment to observe Jerry. He was a fixture in that office – he'd worked his way up from political reporter to editor in the nearly thirty years that he had worked for the paper. He was scowling into his computer screen; she could tell something was not pleasing him. And Jerry felt quite comfortable in sharing his displeasure with all those around him.

Out of the corner of her eye, Mary saw a shadow gliding through the newsroom. She immediately recognized the woman, Anna Paxton, a society columnist who had lived and breathed for her column in the paper. She was a powerful force to be reckoned with in Freeport's high society and she knew it. But she also knew her power was directly related to her column. If she had ever been forced to give up her column, she would be immediately forgotten by those who had wooed her favor for years.

She died at her desk while typing the most malicious comments about a society ingénue's first attempt at a dinner party. That column was replaced by her obituary – which she had kindly penned years before, just in case. She had been quickly replaced, ironically by the same young woman whose societal obituary she had been typing when she died.

Mary didn't know if she remained because that last column was never published, or if she preferred the smell of ink and the clicking of keyboards to the choirs of heavenly angels.

Mary looked at Anna again, recalling some of her unkind columns, and shrugged. Or perhaps, Mary speculated, she was like the Dickens' ghost Marley and in death needed to work off some of the misdeeds performed while she was alive.

The ghost slid across the room, paused next to the editor's office. Mary could feel the enmity vibrating from the specter. As much as Mary would enjoy watching Jerry get spooked, she doubted it would put him in the mood for granting her a favor. She coughed purposefully from her corner. The ghost turned, saw Mary and glowered before she faded into the air.

Jerry, who perhaps was more sensitive than he realized, lifted his head from the computer and looked around.

Here's my chance, Mary thought, and walked across the room to his office.

"Hi, Jerry," she greeted, and was slightly amused to see him jump. "Sorry to disturb you so early in the morning. I was just wondering if I could do some research in the morgue?"

She leaned against the door jamb and smiled. The morgue was actually a large room that housed not only copies of old newspapers, but a computer that held the scanned archives of the paper since the first day it was printed.

Jerry glanced around once more.

"Did…did you see anyone else when you came in?" he asked.

Mary shrugged. "I would venture to say that you and I are the only living creatures in the building right now."

Mary bit back a smile as Jerry's eyes widened at her comment.

"You see any ghosts in here?" he asked, knowing her reputation.

Mary smiled innocently.

"Come on, Jerry," she answered. "You don't believe in ghosts, right?"

Jerry took a deep breath.

"Yeah, right, ghosts – hogwash, a bunch of crap if you ask me."

Mary nodded. "Absolutely. And you sure wouldn't want to be thinking about them when you were sitting all alone in this old dark building. I mean, if you did believe, it could be really creepy in here."

Jerry glared at her.

"You know where the morgue is, don't you?"

Mary nodded.

"Then go and do whatever you have to do and stop wasting my time."

Mary grinned.

"Thanks Jerry, I appreciate it."

As she turned, Jerry stopped her.

"Hey, O'Reilly, you working on anything interesting?"

Oh, he'd love an unsolved murder case, Mary thought. But there was no way he was getting any information from her.

She turned back and shook her head.

"Just some boring research," she said with a shrug. "But if I turn up any skeletons in the morgue, I'll let you know."

Jerry grunted. "You do that."

As Mary crossed the room and headed toward the morgue, Anna glided past her toward the editor's office with a grin on her face.

Sometimes you have to wait until you're dead for a little payback, Mary thought, *but I'm sure the reward is just as sweet.*

As she stepped into the morgue, all of the lights in the newsroom turned off. Mary heard Jerry's shout of fear, then she closed the door and laughed out loud.

Since the Freeport Republic was the larger paper at the time of the incident, they had more coverage than the Galena paper. The day after Renee's death, her story, considered an accidental drowning, had only made the second page. The first page stories were about the election results and the disappearance of an eight-year-old girl, Jessica Whittaker, who had gone out bicycle riding late that afternoon in the small town of Elizabeth and had never returned.

On the top of the page was a photo of the Ryersons' casting their votes. Below the fold was a picture of Jessica's distraught parents standing in front of their modest home, clutching her school picture. Mary could see the heartache in their eyes and wondered if they ever found their daughter.

She found herself not only searching for information about Renee, but also information about the case of Jessica Whitaker, as she worked through the files that morning. The sun was high in the sky by the time she left the stuffy room that housed the morgue. She had a file filled with information on both cases when she walked back to her office.

Stanley sat outside his store on his bench reading through the paper when Mary approached.

"So, Stanley, what's going on in the world," Mary sat next to him and peeked over his shoulder.

"Well, looks like our police chief's gonna have his way with those parking meters," Stanley said. "No one at the city council meeting opposed his proposal."

"No one in the city council ever goes downtown," Mary said. "What happened to good old fashioned investigation? Doesn't anyone ever look before they leap?"

Stanley grinned.

"Well, I kinda expected you to show up to the meeting and put them all in line."

Mary sighed.

"You know, I would have been there, but I had an appointment," she said. "But you're right; I should have made the time."

"Well, there's still time," Stanley said. "Police Chief said that he'd wait a couple of weeks before he ordered the parking meters, just in case any downtown businessman wanted to talk to him about it."

"Business*man*?" Mary asked.

Stanley's eyes twinkled.

"Yep, I believe those were his words," he chuckled. "Know of any businessmen who might want to talk to the police chief?"

Mary stood up and took a deep breath. "Why this city decided to hire Barney Fife is a mystery to me."

Stanley chuckled. "New police chief didn't look much like Barney Fife to me," he said with a grin. "Nope, but then again, my eye sight's been failing for a long time now."

Mary laughed.

"You have the sharpest eyes of anyone I know," she said, shaking her head. "But I've been a cop, and I can spy a Barney Fife a mile away."

Someone with a deep voice cleared his throat just behind Mary.

Well, crap, Mary thought, *I just know this isn't going to be good.*

Stanley peered around Mary and chuckled. "Why hello there, Chief Alden, we were just talking about you."

Mary glared at Stanley and Stanley looked back at Mary, eyes wide with innocence.

Mary bit her lip and shut her eyes in mortification for just a moment. She exhaled deeply. Okay, time to put on her big girl pants and take it like a woman. "Hi, I'm Mary…"

The words froze on her lips.

"You!" they said in astonished unison.

The police chief was the first to recover. He grinned. "You know, I've always considered myself as more of an Andy Taylor kind of guy. By the way, I missed our race this morning."

Chapter Six

So I finally meet my mystery jogger and she ends up being Mary O'Reilly the nut case, Police Chief Bradley Alden thought as he continued down Main Street. *Why are the cute ones always psycho?*

He thought about the look on her face when she finally turned around. He chuckled. The look was priceless. And the Barney Fife line. He had to admit it was funny.

He scanned the street that made up one fifth of downtown Freeport. She was right, though, he hadn't taken the time to find out more about downtown. The mayor had suggested the parking meters and, thinking the mayor knew the town better than he did, had just agreed. What the hell was the mayor thinking? Parking meters would only drive business away from an already struggling shopping district.

He crossed the street and headed up State Street to Stephenson. There were more businesses on Stephenson and they looked to be thriving, but with the onset of the big box stores at the other side of town, he knew these mom-and-pop retail stores were fighting to keep their heads above water.

Up and down most of the downtown streets he had also noticed a number of empty storefronts, scattered amongst the other shops.

So how did he go back to the mayor and tell him that he was out of his mind?

Bradley shook his head. He really hated politics.

"Got a lot on your mind?" Stanley asked, walking up alongside him.

"You set her up," Bradley said, continuing his slow pace down the street.

"Naw, I wouldn't do that," Stanley grinned, falling in alongside him. "Course, if I happen to enjoy when a series of ironic coincidences happens right in front of me, you can't blame a man.

"Sides, I figured it was time the two of you met," he said.

"Why's that?" Bradley asked, stopping to turn and look at Stanley.

"You're a couple of the few people in town with any common sense," Stanley said. "Thought you might want to work together."

"A woman who sees ghosts for a living?" Bradley asked. "She has common sense?"

Stanley chuckled. "Guess you got a little more learning to do, Chief."

Bradley shook his head and started walking again. "I've got more things to worry about than Mary O'Reilly."

Stanley chuckled again. "Just tell the mayor that the traffic downtown will never recoup the initial cost of the parking meters. Fiscally responsible, that always makes them feel good."

Bradley stopped again. "What? You read minds and she sees spirits?"

Stanley laughed. "See you're learning already."

Stanley put his hand on Bradley's arm. "This is where I leave you," he said. "You seemed to be too smart of a man to judge a person on the gossip of others."

Bradley smiled. "That was a back-handed compliment if I ever heard one."

Stanley nodded. "Don't disappoint me."

Bradley watched Stanley walk into the coffee shop and have every one of the young waitresses stop what they were doing to fawn over him. "He's simply amazing." Bradley smiled.

He turned and continued down the street. A pregnant woman with long brown hair stepped out of the bakery a few doors ahead of him. Bradley caught his breath and quickened his pace to catch her. *Jeannine!*

She didn't move like Jeannine, but that could have changed during the time she'd been gone. Had she come to Freeport? Was she looking for him?

He was nearly jogging when the woman stopped to look into a shop window. He saw her profile. His stomach clenched. It wasn't Jeannine. Damn.

He took a deep breath. When would he finally stop looking for her? When would he move on?

Besides, he reasoned, *she wouldn't be pregnant anymore. I'd have a daughter. Our daughter. She would be eight years old. If she's alive. If they're both alive.*

He ran a hand across his forehead and leaned against one of the empty storefronts. He had to get a grip on himself before the people in town thought he was as loony as Mary O'Reilly. He shrugged. Maybe she wasn't that loony – he saw ghosts everywhere he went, too.

Chapter Seven

"So, after you pulled your foot out of your mouth, what did you say?" Rosie asked, sitting on the edge of Mary's desk and munching on a bag of mini carrots.

Mary shrugged. "I don't know…something."

Stanley chuckled. "I remember exactly what you said."

"Stanley, really, you don't need to help," Mary said emphatically.

"No, I think Rosie needs to understand how you stood up to that police chief for the good of all of the small businesses downtown."

Rosie raised her eyebrows as she crunched another carrot. "Really," she munched. "Wow. Good for you, Mary. What did she say?"

"Stanley, please," Mary pleaded.

"She stood right up to that police chief and said… Now Mary, pay attention and make sure I have this right… She said, 'Damn it!' and then she walked away. Did I get that right, Mary?"

"Good one, Mary," Rosie laughed, "I always knew you had a way with words."

"Thanks for the support, Stanley," Mary said. "Where would I be without my friends?"

"You know, I believe that police chief's single," Stanley said to Rosie, ignoring Mary's comments.

"Is that so?" Rosie asked, her eyebrows rising even further. "Was he that very good-looking young man in uniform walking down the street earlier? Had the look of a young Burt Lancaster?"

"Yes, the very one," Stanley replied.

"Well, well," Rosie said, her gaze turning to Mary.

"Yes, that's what I thought too," Stanley said, nodding in agreement.

"Excuse me," Mary said throwing her arms up in the air, "I don't think I asked for any help with my private affairs."

"That's the problem," Stanley snorted, "you ain't having any private affairs."

"Stanley! I can't believe you just said that."

"I'm old – not dead."

"A young Burt Lancaster," Rosie sighed and closed her eyes, hugging herself. "I can still picture the beach scene in *From Here To Eternity*."

She shivered. "It still gives me palpitations."

Mary shook her head. "Okay, that's enough; some of us have work to do."

"Are you asking us to leave?" Stanley asked.

"No, I'm kicking you out. Asking would be too nice."

Stanley chuckled. "Good of you to be subtle about it."

Rosie sniffed. "I'm only going because I have good manners, unlike some people."

"Bye. Don't let the door hit you…"

The door closed with a snap and Mary collapsed into her chair, trying to control a grin as Stanley and Rosie walked past her picture window and waved.

"Good grief, and they're supposed to be more mature," she laughed as she turned around to face her desk. She opened the manila envelope Susan had given her the night before and started to scan the content into her computer. As each new document appeared on the screen she gave it a cursory look and then saved it to a computer file. Just as she was clicking on the "Save" button on the next to the last document, a name caught her eye, "Jerry Wiley."

"Well, Jerry, what were you up to twenty-four years ago?" she muttered as she pulled the original document out of the scanner. Jerry's name was included in the list of those attending the party that night. But he wasn't just an invited guest; Jerry was listed as a member of the Senator's campaign team.

"Well, just look at this," Mary murmured as she read further down the list. "This list is getting more and more interesting."

Other than poor Renee, the other members of the campaign team seemed to have done very well for themselves. Jerry Wiley, assistant campaign manager – now editor in chief of the paper. Mike Steele, campaign fund raiser – now president of Freeport National Bank. Hank Montague, campaign manager

61

– now chair of the local Republican Party and mayor of Freeport.

She looked down the list of the other guests, it read like a who's-who of local power brokers. Even though Mary was a recent resident of the area, she could recognize most of the names because of their frequent appearance in the paper.

She needed to know more about the people on this list than a few quotes. She needed dirt – and she knew just the ghost to give it to her. Glancing at the clock on her computer screen, she saw it was almost four o'clock. The newsroom would be crowded with reporters. She'd have to wait until later tonight to get what she needed. In the meantime she would follow some other leads to find out just what it was about Renee Peterson that made someone want to kill her.

The small subdivision was just west of Freeport in the rural portion of Stephenson County. By larger city standards it wouldn't have even been considered a subdivision, just a scattering of a dozen small homes with large yards and a few cul-de-sacs. Mary drove her car slowly down the road, not only observing the twenty-five mph speed limit, but also watching for the address in the dimming evening light.

Once she found the right house, she parked her car and smiled at the view. Four not-too-scary jack-o-lanterns guarded the front steps. Colorful Mums bloomed in the tiny front garden, and ghosts and goblins hung in the front window. She was sorry that she didn't have a trick or treat bag with her because she was sure this would be one of the houses that gave out really good candy. This was a house that understood kids.

She climbed the stairs and knocked on the screen door. Immediately she heard a dog's excited bark and the clicking of paws against wood floor.

"Jackson, down," the woman's voice commanded from the other side of the door. "Andy, grab Jackson."

Mary heard a slipping sound and a thump, and then the door was opened by a woman she guessed to be in her late forties. The woman smiled and extended her hand. "Hi, I'm Lisa Merrill."

Just past her a large Golden Retriever was on its back next to a small decorative table that was lying on its side. A young man, probably in his early twenties, knelt next to him trying to stand the table up again and control the dog at the same time. But when the dog saw Mary, he quickly rolled over, righted himself and lunged at the door.

"Jackson, sit," Mary commanded. Jackson stopped mid-lunge, dropped his large haunches immediately to the ground and looked up to Mary with adoring eyes and a lolling tongue.

"How in the world did you do that?" the young man asked, pulling himself up from the floor.

"A trick I learned in a past life," Mary replied. "Hi, I'm Mary O'Reilly."

"Great trick. Please come in," Lisa said and then, motioning to the young man, explained, "This is my son, Robbie."

"Jackson never listens to us," Robbie said. "The trainer said that he has a greeting disorder."

Mary laughed and patted Jackson's big head. "So you have a greeting disorder do you? Well, you make up for it in personality."

Jackson wagged his tail and tried to scoot closer to Mary.

"Robbie, why don't you put Jackson out in the backyard while I visit with Miss O'Reilly?"

"Sure, Mom," Robbie agreed.

Lisa led Mary into a simply furnished living room. "I've heard about you. You do private investigation, right?"

Mary nodded. "Yes, I have an office in the old Hawthorne Building."

"That's a great old building," Lisa said. "Good place for an office. So, what did you want to talk to me about?"

"I wanted to ask you about Renee Peterson," Mary said, watching Lisa for an initial reaction.

Lisa sat back on the couch and clasped her hands together tightly. "Renee Peterson," she said softly. "Wow. That really takes me back."

"She and I were roommates. I was going to school part time and working at JC Penney. Renee was working for the senator, on his campaign."

"What kind of roommate was she?"

Lisa shrugged. "I don't know, we were both young and fairly easy-going. If the dishes didn't get done right away, no one cared. But I always knew I could count on her and I think she knew she could count on me."

"On the night she died, what do you remember?"

"She seemed so excited about the party," Lisa said. "She went into town early to have a couple of last minute alterations to her dress."

She shook her head and looked directly at Mary. "For the longest time I blamed myself. I mean, what if it hadn't been an accident? What if she killed herself? Shouldn't I have been able to tell if she was depressed? Shouldn't I have been able to stop her before she committed suicide?"

Mary leaned forward. "What if it wasn't accidental or a suicide?"

Lisa's eyes widened. "But then, that would mean..."

"That someone killed her," Mary supplied, sitting back in her chair.

Lisa was confused. "Why would anyone want to kill her? She wouldn't have hurt anyone. She was so sweet, so..."

"So in love with the senator?" Mary supplied.

Lisa looked surprised. She studied Mary for a moment and nodded. "Yes, she was very much in love with Ryerson. But she wasn't, you know, promiscuous."

"Did she have other relationships?" Mary asked. "An old boyfriend or someone who was interested in her?"

"No," Lisa said, "she was pretty sheltered. I don't think she dated much in high school or in college, for that matter. She was pretty mature for her age. I think Ryerson was her, um, first, if you know what I mean. She really loved him."

"What did you think about the relationship?"

Lisa shrugged. "Okay, well, I didn't really know the man; I only knew what Renee told me. But I didn't think too highly of a guy who slept with one of his employees behind his wife's back. I mean, really, that's just sleazy."

"Did Renee think it was sleazy?"

"Oh, no, she thought he was wonderful. She said he was going to leave his wife for her."

"Did she think the baby would make a difference?"

Lisa froze. "How did you know that she was pregnant?"

Mary shrugged, quietly pleased that Lisa had indeed confirmed the pregnancy. "It's what I do."

Lisa nodded reluctantly. "Yeah, she found out on election day. She got one of those home pregnancy kits because she had missed her period, but she didn't want anyone to know."

"So she told him?"

Lisa shrugged. "I don't know. She said that she was going to tell him after the party."

"Did anyone else know about it?"

Lisa shook her head. "No, I'm sure she wouldn't have told anyone else. She would have never jeopardized Ryerson's future."

"Perhaps someone else who worked on the campaign with them, someone she could trust?"

"No, she didn't really get along with the other members of the campaign team. They were from the good old boys club and treated her like their personal secretary rather than Ryerson's assistant. She wouldn't have told them."

"Did Renee and Ryerson have any special place they met?"

Lisa thought for a moment. "Yeah, there was some garden in the back of the estate. It was a little way from the house. It was a hidden garden with a heated pool. She told me they would sneak away and meet there all the time. She called it their secret paradise."

"That's where they found her," Lisa continued, her eyes widening in understanding. "I hadn't put it together before, but that's where she drowned.

"Do you think that he...?" She stopped and put her hand over her mouth. "All these years, why didn't anyone investigate her death?"

"Because everyone assumed that she drowned," Mary said.

"I can't believe it," Lisa said. "What will her parents think?"

Mary moved forward in her chair. "Lisa, I haven't spoken with her parents yet," Mary explained. "At this point, I'm hesitant to do so until I can find more concrete information about the case. Do you understand?"

Lisa nodded. "Yeah, why bring something up if you can't prove it," she said. "They would just have to relive her death again."

"Exactly," Mary said. "I know you kept Renee's confidence about her pregnancy for all of these years. Can you keep this confidence until I learn more?"

"Yes. Yes, I can," she said. "You're going to figure this out, aren't you? You'll find out who did this."

Mary nodded. "I promise."

Chapter Eight

Mary pulled up to the front of her office and parked. Although it seemed a little dramatic, she had dressed in all black to be sure she didn't attract attention.

Mary acknowledged the downtown area had a different feeling at night. The stores were closed, the people were gone, just buildings that sat waiting for the next day to come. Even the shadows of the past were different: the distraught teen waiting at the Greyhound Bus Stop, the secretary and her boss sneaking out a side door, and the broken-down drunk sipping from his brown paper sack. The shadows only appeared for a moment and then faded away like mist in a field. It was all slightly creepy.

She locked her car and headed down Main Street. She'd decided that parking in front of her office and walking made more sense. She didn't want anyone asking questions about why her very distinct car was parked in the Freeport Republic lot at one a.m.

She jumped when she caught someone lurking behind a streetlight post. "Damned scarecrows," she swore when she realized the stalker was made of plywood.

She walked to the back of the building and pulled herself up on the loading dock. She knew the building would be locked, but because her contact had had a penchant for smoking, she figured Anna would find her way out to the dock for a cigarette break.

Mary settled herself on a stack of pallets and leaned back against the wall. She didn't have to wait too long. In a matter of moments, Anna Paxton glided out of the building and hovered over the dock.

"Anna," Mary called and was amused to have startled the ghost. "I have a deal for you."

"Why would I want to deal with a second-rate private eye?" she sneered. "You aren't even in my league."

"Hey, you give me information and I give you the scoop of a lifetime," Mary said, hoping Anna wouldn't realize that giving her a scoop would do her absolutely no good.

Anna eyed Mary with suspicion. "What kind of scoop?"

"Okay Anna, here's the deal: do you want the scoop or not?" Mary shrugged. "Hey, it's okay. I can always ask your replacement."

An angry hiss escaped the ghostly form and she moved closer. "She's nothing but a no-talent bitch," Anna sneered. "She doesn't deserve a scoop."

Mary shrugged. "Yeah, well, if I can't have the best, I'll have to settle for the imitator."

Anna slowly smiled. "Yessss, that's what she is – an imitator. Trying to be me, trying to replace me. No one can do that."

Mary glanced down at the list of names she brought and thought she'd try one.

"I don't know, Jerry Wiley sure seems to think she has what it takes."

One and a half hours later Mary walked back to her car with a notebook filled with venomous comments, snide innuendoes and really juicy gossip. She hoped that she would be able to dissect it and find some threads of truth.

She walked back to her office and put the information in her files. She glanced at the clock – it was two-forty-five. There was no way she was going to get up and run in the morning.

Then she thought about the Chief of Police. She thought about his smirk. His Andy Taylor comment. Her lack of response to any of those.

"If I don't show, he's going to think he intimidated me. And damn it, I'm not going to let anyone think that."

The alarm clock rang less than two hours later. Mary moaned, but forced herself out of bed. She grabbed the diet cola she had left out the night before. "This is so bad for me," she admitted as she guzzled down her caffeine fix.

Pulling open the top drawer, she grabbed her running gear.

"We'll just show him that Mary O'Reilly isn't a pushover."

Mary jogged into the park looking for a fight. *Just let him say something smart*, she thought irritably, *I'll kick him back to Mayberry, police chief or not.*

Her mood brightened a little when she saw his surprise as she jogged toward the carousel. "Yeah, didn't think I'd show up, did you," she murmured to herself. "I showed you."

"I'm sorry, I didn't hear what you said," Bradley said, looking confused.

Mary glared at him. "I wasn't talking to you."

"Oh," he nodded understandingly. "Are we in the presence of ghosts?"

Mary studied him for a moment. Yes, there was mocking in his voice. Yes, he thought he was pretty superior. And yes, she was really pissed off.

"Yeah, Andy Taylor's standing behind you and he wants to kick your ass," she replied. "Are you ready to race?"

"Yeah, but I..." he began.

"Good," Mary interrupted and sped down the path. She was enjoying the look of shocked surprise on his face for a few moments until she could hear the sound of his footfalls gaining on her.

"Crap."

Mary pushed forward and kept ahead of him for another mile, but she could feel the effects of a mostly sleepless night taking hold. The muscles in her legs began to shake and she knew she was going to lose this race. She finally slowed down to a jog and waited for him to pass her.

"Well, at least the view will be nice when he passes. He might be an idiot, but he has cute buns."

Mary chuckled.

"So, what's so funny?"

She was surprised to see Bradley keeping time with her slower pace.

"I thought you'd have passed me and been all the way to the finish line by now," she said.

He shrugged. "Yeah, well, I didn't get a whole lot of sleep last night. Someone reported seeing a cat burglar prowling the streets of downtown last night, so I was on stake out."

"A cat burglar, huh?" she asked with a gulp.

"Yeah, they said it was just like that movie with Angelina Jolie. How did he put it? 'A total babe dressed in all black.'"

Mary grinned. "Angelina Jolie, huh?"

He nodded. "Yep, the funny thing about it – she had a car just like yours and it was parked in front of your office."

Crap! Busted, she thought.

"Wow, that is funny," she replied, trying her best to look unconcerned.

"So, why are you so tired this morning?" he asked.

Mary knew a set-up when she saw one.

"I didn't see you follow me home," she said, dropping from a jog to a walk.

At least he had the decency to look slightly ashamed when he grinned. "Well, yeah, I stayed about half a block behind you and kept my lights off."

"You know that's against the law," Mary stated.

"I was willing to risk it," he replied.

Mary laughed; she couldn't help herself.

"I can assure you that what I was doing last night had nothing to do with burglary," she told him.

He nodded. "I didn't think it did. Are you working on a case?"

"Yes," she answered.

"You want to talk about it?"

"Not yet," she said, "but when the time's right I promise I'll call you in. I do have respect for the law."

"Even if it's being represented by Barney Fife?" he asked stopping and blocking her way on the path.

Mary blushed. "Okay, for that I apologize," she said.

He grinned. "Apology accepted. Shall we start over?"

Mary nodded.

"Hi, I'm Bradley Alden, the new police chief," he said, extending his hand.

She smiled and shook his hand. "Mary O'Reilly, private investigator. It's nice to meet you."

The quick click of the handcuff over her wrist had her pulling back in shock.

"What the...?"

Bradley shrugged apologetically. "Sorry, there's a warrant out on you for trespassing and planting an explosive device. I've got to take you in."

He gently took her other arm and clapped the handcuff on her other wrist. He started reading her the Miranda Rights.

"Planting an explosive? What the hell?" she snapped. "I never…"

"Yeah, well, let's do this by the book, so we can figure out what's happening."

Mary turned to him. "You don't really think…"

Bradley looked into Mary's eyes. "I've had lots of experience in law enforcement. I've had military experience. And I've done my share in special ops. I think I would have recognized a terrorist if I'd been running with one every day for six months. Do you understand what I'm saying?"

Mary nodded. He finished her Miranda Rights and led her to his cruiser.

"Besides," he added. "The bomb was put together like an amateur did it. If you'd have done it, it would have been professional."

Mary grinned. "Damn straight!"

Ten minutes later Mary sat in the regulation metal and vinyl chair next to his desk and did the best she could to answer the questions.

"Were you on the loading docks at the Freeport Republic last night at approximately one a.m.?"

Mary knew enough about law enforcement to realize that unless they had her fingerprints or an eye witness, they would never even ask her the questions – so, as usual, honesty was the best policy.

"Yes, I was on the loading dock at the Freeport Republic last night."

"What were you doing there?" he asked, motioning with a look to the recorder on his desk, so she didn't give him a smart-ass answer.

"I was interviewing a source for some information in a case I'm working on," she replied.

"What is the name of your source?"

She shook her head. "I believe that the names of my sources are protected under the 2nd Amendment to the Constitution."

Bradley smiled. "Good try, but that's only if you're a journalist, not a private investigator."

"I was at the newspaper office," she tried. "Shouldn't that count?"

He just shook his head.

Mary shrugged. "Well, you're not going to like my next answer any better."

"Try me."

"I was speaking with Anna Paxton, the former society columnist of the Freeport Republic."

Bradley looked confused. "Why wouldn't I like that answer? Now we have a witness who can verify where you were and what you did."

"Because Anna Paxton died about twelve months ago."

Bradley stood up and slammed his hand on the desk. "Dammit, Mary, this isn't the time to be funny. Explosives. Bombs. Those go under the category of Homeland Security, and they don't play games."

Mary took a deep breath and stood up to face Bradley.

"I'm not being funny, I don't play games, I understand this is serious – but I actually am able to communicate with ghosts."

Bradley ran his hand through his hair. "Come on, Mary, you can trust me. I know you use this 'ghost thing' as a marketing ploy, but you can tell me the truth."

Mary took another deep breath, this one to prevent her from socking Bradley in the arm.

"Yep, you got me. I mean, being an honorably decorated ex-cop, part of the vice squad and up for promotion to detective status, as well as graduating with honors in criminal justice, wasn't enough experience to start my own P.I. agency. Yep, I needed a spin, so I just thought I'd throw in that I can see dead people," she fumed. "Yep, that would keep the kooks away."

Bradley sat down with a thump. "You mean to tell me that you actually believe that you can talk to ghosts?"

Mary leaned over his desk. "Not only do I believe it, Chief Alden, I actually *do* talk with ghosts."

Chapter Nine

Damn, she wasn't a nut.

Bradley hung up the phone and leaned back in his chair. Who would have guessed that Mary O'Reilly had really been a top-notch Chicago police officer? Not him.

Her commanding officer had nothing but good things to say about his former employee. She really had been on the fast track to becoming a detective and she deserved it. Smart, intuitive and dedicated. Who would have guessed?

So what was all this crazy talk about seeing ghosts? No one sees ghosts because there are no such things as ghosts.

He had even asked her C.O. about the ghost thing, but the guy had enough Irish in him to believe in that kind of crap. But even he admitted that at first they sent Mary in to speak with the department shrink. But she turned the shrink into a believer, especially when she had delivered a message from her dead mother.

He remembered the seething anger in Mary's eyes when he clipped those handcuffs on her. Her C.O. wasn't the only one with a lot of Irish. He was glad she wasn't packing.

Okay, that wasn't fair. It had been pretty underhanded of him to trick her like that. He could only barely justify it because he didn't know how she would react to being arrested. And he had to give her points, she had been honest with him. At least she was honest within her own strange little fantasy world.

Planting bombs. No, she wasn't planting bombs. He'd stake his job on that one. Besides, the forensic guys pulled the whole bomb apart and couldn't find anything linking Mary to it. She was set up. But why?

Someone playing a gag? Someone giving out a little payback?

He needed more information to figure out this puzzle. He sighed deeply, knowing there was only one way he was going to get it.

Chapter Ten

Mary had a splitting headache. She sat at the desk in her office, cradling her head in her hands and wishing the world would go away.

She would always remember the look Bradley gave her as he solicitously escorted her out of his office and asked one of his deputies to see her safely home. He even patted her arm and told her she needn't worry; he would make sure everything was taken care of.

"He patted my arm, like I was a nut," she growled. "He patted my freakin' arm."

She dropped her head on the desk and laid there. She heard the door open and close, but she just didn't care.

"Hmmm, hard at work I see," Rosie said casually.

"Nothing like putting your head into it," Stanley added.

"Go away," Mary groaned. "Can't you see I'm trying to be depressed?"

Mary could hear chairs being pulled toward her desk, so she closed her eyes.

"I can't see you, so you're not there," she said.

"Funny, people say that a lot about ghosts too," Rosie said.

"That's not funny," Mary sulked.

"I heard the police chief hauled your butt to the hoosegow," Stanley said. "What did you do, call him more names?"

Mary covered her head with her arms. "What did I do to deserve this?" she cried.

"Now, Mary, it's time to put on your big girl pants and get back to work," Rosie chided. "Don't you have a case to work on?"

Mary nodded from under her arms.

"Never thought of you as a quitter," Stanley added.

Mary sighed. "I'm usually not."

"We brought you some cinnamon rolls from Coles Bakery," Rosie added.

Mary immediately raised her head. "I love you guys."

"And a large diet cola," Stanley added. "That should take care of your headache."

Mary felt like crying. "I don't deserve you two."

Rosie grinned. "Yeah, we know. But don't worry, you'll make it up to us."

They all laughed.

Mary took a big bite of the cinnamon roll and sighed, "This tastes like heaven."

"You'd know," Stanley quipped.

Mary chuckled. "You know he thinks I'm nuts? He patted my arm and had a deputy escort me home."

Rosie snorted. "Well, at least you're not in jail."

"What did he bust you for anyway?" Stanley asked.

"Trying to blow up the Freeport Republic building," Mary answered.

"Well, I agree the editorials have been a little off lately, but blowing the place up seems a little extreme," Rosie said.

"I didn't try to blow it up," Mary explained. "I met with Anna Paxton to ask her some questions about a case I'm working on. I left the dock and there were no explosives in sight. Suddenly there's a warrant out for my arrest and they are accusing me of trying to blow up the building. And besides that, the bomb looks like an amateur put it together."

"Well, if you were going to bomb something, you'd be sure to get it done right," Stanley said.

"That's what Bradley said," Mary agreed, biting into the cinnamon roll again.

"Bradley?" Rosie asked. "Who's Bradley?"

Crap. Busted again, Mary thought.

"That's the police chief's name, Bradley Alden," she told them. "He told me his name just before he slapped the handcuffs on me."

"That seems a little rude," Rosie said.

"Yeah, and a little tricky," Mary added. "It was a fairly impressive maneuver."

"Seems to me someone doesn't want you investigating the case you're on," Stanley interjected.

Mary froze halfway into her next bite of cinnamon roll. "Well, duh," she said, shaking her head. "Of course, that's the reason. Stanley, you're brilliant."

"So we'll just leave you to your investigating," Rosie said.

"Go get 'em, girlie," Stanley said, winking at Mary.

"Thanks, thanks a lot," she replied and immediately began searching the notes she had taken the day before.

Several hours later, Mary knew she had to make another trip into Galena and meet with both the senator and Susan Ryerson. She needed to find out if either of them knew about Renee's pregnancy.

After a quick phone call confirming they would both be home, Mary grabbed her notebook, headed out the office door and nearly collided with Police Chief Bradley Alden.

"Sorry, I have an appointment," Mary said, neatly walking around him.

"Mary, wait," he said, catching her arm.

Mary looked pointedly at his hand on her arm and then up at him. "Are you arresting me again?"

"No, I'm not," he replied, releasing her hand. "I would like to ask you a few questions if you don't mind."

"Really? Without handcuffs? What a novel idea."

"Listen, I had no choice, I…"

"Your questions, Chief...? I'm really running late," she interrupted.

He pressed his lips together for a moment, biting back his anger and then nodded.

"Was there anyone else present on the dock when you were there?" he asked. "Let me qualify that, anyone who would leave fingerprints?"

"No, there was no one on the dock with me who would leave fingerprints."

"Why did you choose the dock to conduct this interview?"

"Because my contact stays close to the editorial offices of the paper, but often travels to the dock for an occasional cigarette break."

"Ghosts smoke?" he asked incredulously.

Mary rolled her eyes. "Ghosts are merely the spirits of people who have died," she explained. "If you had a habit while you were alive, why do you think you would change it after you're dead?"

Bradley shrugged. "I guess you wouldn't."

"Anna Paxton couldn't go more than two hours without a smoke break – so I knew that she would head out to the dock sooner or later."

"Why did you wait until one in the morning to speak with Ms. Paxton?"

"Well, hmmm, maybe because I didn't want any of the reporters to see me talking to myself," she answered.

"So you admit you were talking to yourself," he countered.

"No, I was talking to a ghost who cannot be seen or heard by most people," she said. "So when I talk to ghosts, it strongly resembles me talking to myself. Any other questions?"

"Where are you going?"

"I'm going to meet with a client who lives out of town. I plan on being back in town by this evening," she replied. "Now can I ask you a question?"

"Shoot."

"Who initiated the warrant for my arrest?"

Bradley was surprised and suspicious. "Why do you want to know?"

"I'm working on a case that might have ramifications for some people in high places in this town," she replied. "Knowing who did it might make my job easier."

Bradley nodded, that seemed like a fairly straightforward request. "I'll see what I can find out," he promised.

"Thanks, I'd appreciate it," she replied, opening her car door. "Any more questions?"

"Um, just one," he said. "When did you discover you could talk with ghosts?"

Mary climbed in her car, closed the door, turned the key and then rolled down the window. She leaned out and called to Bradley, "Just after I died."

Then she put the car in gear and drove away from the speechless police chief.

Chapter Eleven

Driving down Highway 20, all Mary could think about was her encounter with Bradley. It left her feeling angry and a little vulnerable. Did everyone in town consider her a kook?

She thought about her small circle of friends in town. It boiled down to Stanley and Rosie. "How sad is that?" she murmured. "I've only got two friends."

She started to feel a pity party coming on and shook herself out of it. There were lots of people who would have been her friend if she had just taken some time to get to know them. But being the only person in Illinois, and perhaps the Midwest, who could actually see ghosts and talk to them gave her very little time for socializing.

She didn't know how it worked, but somehow ghosts in need were drawn to her. That was the main reason she left Chicago and moved to Freeport. There were too many ghosts for Mary to handle in Chicago, especially since she was just beginning to figure out the whole ghost thing. Freeport was the right size for a fledgling ghost hunter.

Mary realized she had passed through Stockton and was only twenty minutes away from Galena. She took a couple of deep breaths and tried to clear her mind so she could concentrate on the case before her. The officers she worked with used to call it her "zone." The zone was a state of mind where she was able to mentally slow everything down and take in all of the details. Inconsequential, random events would suddenly have logical patterns. Pieces of information would fit together. The case would open up to her and finally make sense.

She had used it a lot when she was a cop in Chicago. She always felt she was allowing her intuition take over. It was a way to let the things percolating in the back of her mind come forward.

Now when she used it her new abilities combined with her intuition and she received a better connection with the ghost she was trying to help.

Mary concentrated on Renee Peterson. How had Renee felt that day, discovering her pregnancy, wanting to tell her lover, but knowing her news had to take second place to the election?

Wondering if he would reject her, reject the baby? Wondering if she would keep the baby or get an abortion?

She must have had a lot on her mind that night and the world on her shoulders.

Mary slowed to thirty miles per hour as she entered Elizabeth. The road curved around a large bluff and went downhill into the town.

As she entered the town, she thought one of the houses looked familiar. After a moment, she realized it was the house from the photo in the paper. The story about the little girl, Jessica Whittaker, who had disappeared on the same night Renee had died.

That was the house her parents stood in front of, holding her photo. She had lived there.

Suddenly Mary could see Jessica, riding her bike carefully down the street. The town was no longer the Elizabeth she had driven through earlier that week. Now the town appeared as it had been in 1984. Mary pulled her car to the curb, jumped out and ran down the sidewalk to follow the little girl on the bike.

Jessica wove slowly down the sidewalk and turned at the corner. Mary jogged behind her, keeping her in view. She wore her hair in two blonde ponytails and had pink Strawberry Shortcake ribbons streaming from it. She was dressed in pink pedal-pushers and a matching t-shirt.

The street was steep and Mary had to angle her movements to keep from falling, but Jessica seemed to know every bump and curve and directed her bike like a pro. Jessica drove off the sidewalk and onto a path that led into a wooded glen.

Mary paused for a moment, watching the girl maneuver down the dirt path. While she was still in view, Mary saw her stop her bike and look into the woods. Mary started forward, watching the little girl hold a hand to her ear, as if she was trying to hear something being said. Although she understood she was only watching a shadow of the past, Mary couldn't stop herself from running and trying to stop her.

She could see Jessica looking up and talking with someone. Someone taller, certainly an adult, and then she climbed off the bike and walked into the woods.

"No! No!" Mary cried to herself, jogging as quickly as she could down the steep hill. Mary picked up speed when she saw Jessica being lifted up in the air. Jessica was screaming, pounding her little fists against her unknown captor.

"No!" Mary cried aloud breaking into a run. Pain exploded in Mary's head and she fell backward into darkness.

She could hear voices. She could smell grass. Her head was pounding. What the hell happened?

Mary slowly opened her eyes.

"I saw it, I saw it all," said a drawling masculine voice. "She just ran right into the side of the fort. Darndest thing I'd ever seen – it was like she couldn't see it."

"I think she's waking up," a feminine voice uttered.

Then Mary remembered Jessica. She sat up quickly and immediately regretted it, the whole world tilted to the side.

"Take it easy," a deep masculine voice commanded. "You've got a pretty nasty bump on your head. You might have a concussion."

"Ran right straight into the fort, darndest thing," the voice from earlier repeated.

This time, Mary slowly turned her head and found herself looking at the paramedic who was kneeling at her side. "Can you remember anything?" he asked.

I suppose telling him that I was chasing a ghost isn't going to work, she thought.

"I was jogging down the hill and I must have tripped because suddenly I was hurtling down the hill out of control," she lied, reminding herself silently that sometimes honesty wasn't always the best policy. "I must have hit my head."

"How do you feel?" he asked.

"Like someone hit me with a fort," she answered with a small smile.

He chuckled as he shone his flashlight in each of her eyes. "Well, looks like you don't have a concussion. But you aren't going to look as pretty as usual tomorrow morning."

"You can take some OTC pills for pain, so you can sleep tonight – but if you start having any headaches or blurry vision, I want you to get to your doctor right away. Understand?"

"Yes, sir," Mary answered, trying to stop a groan as he helped her on her feet. "How's the fort?"

This time he laughed aloud. "No permanent damage was done. If you had had a harder head, well, we'd be asking you for your insurance card."

Mary chuckled. "That's a relief."

He helped her over to his truck. "How about if I give you a lift back to your car? That way you won't have to try this hill again."

"I would really appreciate it," Mary replied earnestly, not sure she could make the climb up the hill and back down the street to the car.

"Cool fort," she said to the paramedic. "Well, not so cool up close – but it looks like it's been around for a long time."

"Naw," the paramedic responded. "It was just built in the early nineties. Some local guy got the idea that it should be reconstructed. They brought in an architect and everything. Then they built it with tools that they would have used back when the fort was initially built – to be historically correct."

"Wow, that's great," she replied. "So what was there before the fort was built?"

"A meadow and some woods," he said. "Oh, and an old shed that had been empty for decades. When I was a kid we would swear that it was haunted."

"Really?" she said, knowing that children were often more perceptive to paranormal activity than they realized. "Who did you think haunted it?"

He laughed nervously. "I don't know, it was just kid stuff," he said. "You know, too much imagination and not enough sense."

"I've had experiences like that too," Mary said. "Sometimes it's not just your imagination."

The paramedic pulled his truck to the curb behind Mary's Roadster. He turned in his seat, facing her. "Do you honestly think it could be real?"

"I know it can be real," she said. "What did you see?"

He hesitated.

"It could be important," she added.

"Well, when I was just a kid – maybe ten years old – we were playing 'catch one – catch all' one summer night," he said. "They had just started the excavation on the fort and there were all kinds of cool hiding places down there."

"Even though all the kids thought it was a creepy place, I knew if I hid down there, no one would find me," he said with a grin. "I love to win."

Mary chuckled.

"So anyway, I'm down there hiding behind some of the big logs they had brought in when I hear someone crying," he paused for a moment. "It sounded like my little sister and I think she's in trouble, so I follow the sound. I see this little girl sitting on the ground and she's crying her eyes out. I get maybe ten feet away from her and she looks up and sees me. I stop in my tracks because even though she's there I can see right through her. I mean, she's a ghost."

The paramedic took a deep breath and then continued.

"Then she gets up and motions to me, like to follow her. I can't believe that I had the balls to do it – but, you know, you're kinda in the moment. So I follow her and she leads me to the edge of the old woods. Then three other little girls come out of the woods – you know, just like her. She runs and joins them and then they all just fade away.

"Damn," he swore, rubbing his arms up and down, "still gives me goose bumps."

"Do you remember what they looked like?" Mary asked. "Any of them?"

"Yeah, I'll never forget," he said. "They were all about the same age – like eight – the age of my sister. Because it was getting dark, I couldn't tell the exact color of their hair – but it was dark, you know, like brown or black."

"None of them were blondes?" she asked.

He shook his head. "No, none of them," he replied. "Why?"

"Nothing, just seemed strange that none of them were blondes," she answered.

He shrugged. "Yeah, I guess so,"

"What you saw," she said, "it was real. It was their way of asking for help. Now that you've told their story, someone can help them. Thank you."

Chapter Twelve

Once behind the wheel of her car, she made a quick call to the Ryersons explaining that she would have to meet with them the next day. She had been tempted to go back to the fort and see if she could find the girls herself, but since her head was pounding, the sun was setting and she wasn't too sure she could walk in a straight line, she opted for home.

When Mary finally pulled the Roadster into her driveway, she was not pleased to see Bradley's car parked in front of her house. "Great. Just what I need – another show down," she muttered.

She grabbed her purse and her notebook and exited the car. The world tilted when she tried to stand up and she had to grab on to the car to keep from falling. Her head was pounding and her legs felt like rubber.

"Crap," she whispered, sweat beading on her forehead.

Seconds later she heard a car door close behind her.

"Mary, I need to talk to you," Bradley called.

She didn't even try to turn around. Putting all of the strength she had in sounding normal, she answered, "Not tonight, Bradley, I have a headache."

Unfortunately, he was not deterred. "Mary, this is important," he persisted.

She turned quickly, stumbled and fell against the hood of the car. "Damn it, Bradley, either arrest me or just leave me the hell alone."

"Mary! Look at your face! What happened to you? Were you mugged?"

Before she could react, Bradley was next to her, his arm around her waist, half-carrying her to his vehicle. "I'm taking you to the Emergency Room."

"Bradley, leave me alone," she said, pushing against his shoulders and his chest.

Suddenly the vision of little Jessica Whittaker pounding against the unknown attacker's chest came to mind and Mary felt sick to her stomach. "Bradley," she groaned, "stop. Right now!"

Bradley looked down at Mary. The request this time was more of a plea. Her face was ashen and she looked like she was going to... Bradley quickly helped her down to the grass, next to the curb. She leaned over and emptied her stomach all over his white-walled tires.

He held her shoulders and, when she was done, helped her sit up. "Stay right there."

I couldn't move if I wanted to, Mary thought.

Bradley reached into his car and pulled out a bottle of water and a couple of wet wipes. Her hands were shaking as she swallowed a little water, but they were steadier as she wiped her face and the back of her neck. She took a shuddering deep breath and laid her head in her hands.

"You okay?" Bradley asked, kneeling by her side.

"Yeah, I think so," she said softly.

"You barfed on official police department property," he teased gently.

She chuckled weakly. "Probably better than barfing on the official police chief."

"You have a point. So, you want to tell the official police chief what happened?"

"I ran into a fort," she replied with a half-groan.

He looked over at the Roadster. "You were in a car accident?"

"No, the car was parked. I ran into a fort."

"Was it hiding?"

"No, I just didn't see it because I was in the past."

Bradley was silent for a moment.

"Oh, okay, I understand," he said, his voice clearly insinuating that he didn't understand.

Mary shook her head and was immediately sorry. "No, you don't understand," she said, "and damn it, I'm too tired to explain, okay?"

Once again she found herself supported by a pair of strong arms and half-carried toward her house. But this time she was too tired and sore to argue. She just laid her head against his shoulder and enjoyed breathing in his very male scent.

Bradley helped her climb the porch stairs, which seemed much higher than ever before, and stood at the front door. "Mary, what's your code?" he asked, looking at her keyless entry.

She looked like she was going to argue. "Damn it, Mary, I'm the police chief. And you can change it later if you'd like."

She told him the code and he punched it in, while he held her against him.

"If I wasn't so tired, I'd be really impressed with this show of manly strength."

Bradley chuckled.

"Oh, crap, did I say that out loud?" she asked, mortified.

Bradley laughed.

"Yes, I suppose I did."

He opened the door and carried her into her living room, setting her gently on the couch. "Stay," he ordered.

She could hear him rummaging around in her kitchen. In a few moments he was back, carrying a plastic bag filled with ice cubes and a dish towel to wrap it in.

"If I could find a steak, I would have brought it. But this will do for now," he said.

"I have a black eye?" Mary squealed, trying to sit up and look into a mirror.

Bradley held her down. "Trust me; you don't look bad, really."

"You don't lie often, do you, Chief?" Mary sniffed.

"Come on, after my display of manly strength, you can certainly call me Bradley."

She laughed, but it hurt and she winced. He handed her some pain pills from her cabinet and a glass of water. She willingly swallowed them. "Thanks."

"You need to see a doctor," Bradley said.

"The nice paramedic said that I didn't have a concussion and that I just needed to rest," she replied.

The lack of sleep from the prior night and the long day was catching up with her. Mary could barely keep her eyes open.

"A paramedic had to look you over?"

"Well, he was there when I woke up," she yawned.

"You fainted?" Bradley's voice was getting more and more agitated.

"No, I think I knocked myself out," Mary said wearily. "I don't remember much after running into the fort."

"You're telling me that you actually ran, like *running* ran, into a fort?"

"Well, it was a meadow at the time," she replied, her eyes slowly closing.

"Is it me or are you not making any sense?" he asked, looking down at Mary sleeping soundly on the couch. "Well, damn."

# # # #

The wind ruffled the sheer curtains that swept over the polished wood floor. Bradley slept in the recliner next to the couch, keeping vigil over Mary. In the hall, the antique grandfather clock struck midnight. Clear tones echoed the twelve chimes throughout the quiet house. Bradley woke, instinctively knowing something was different.

Silence shrouded the room for a moment. Then a muffled noise came from behind the basement door. *Thump. Thump. Thump.*

It moved closer. The doorknob rattled. Bradley pulled his service revolver from his holster and slowly, carefully walked toward the basement door. *Thump. Thump. Thump.*

The door shook from the force of the blows, the damaged brass lock couldn't hold and the door crashed open.

"Freeze, Police," Bradley yelled, his revolver stretched out in front of him, his stanch lethal.

"Bradley, what's going on?" Mary called.

"Stay put," Bradley commanded, as he dove over the counter, bringing a large cookie jar with him, and rolled to face the basement stairs.

The doorway was empty. He plastered himself against the wall and investigated all of the corners of the kitchen.

"Bradley, what in the world have you done to my cookie jar?" Mary asked, her drowsy expression filled with confusion, as she entered the kitchen.

Bradley dashed through the kitchen, pulled Mary into his arms and pushed her behind him. "I told you to stay put," he growled.

"While you destroy my kitchen? I don't think so," she replied.

"Mary, there is an intruder in your house," he whispered ferociously. "An intruder."

Mary tried to look past him to the clock on the stove, but couldn't. "What time is it?" she finally asked.

Bradley was stunned. "Didn't you hear me? There is an intruder in your home."

"Yes, I heard you," she replied and then repeated slowly, "What time is it?"

"It's about five after twelve," he said.

"Oh, okay, it's Lieutenant Earl Belvidere," she said, yawning and leaning against the counter. "Once he realizes that I'm not upstairs, he'll come on back down."

"What the hell?" Bradley asked.

"Shhhh, you'll scare him."

Bradley stood still and could hear footsteps above them.

"How the hell?"

"Shhhhh," Mary insisted, moving toward the stairs.

Bradley moved so he was shielding Mary, his gun still drawn. He heard the footsteps on the staircase, but he couldn't see anything. The sounds moved directly past him, but no one was there. He thought he caught a whiff of the sickly sweet smell of rotting flesh, but it was gone as quickly as it had come.

The basement door across the kitchen closed by itself, the broken lock tumbled to the floor and echoed in the now silent kitchen. Only then did he hear the retreating thumping sounds on the stairs. Then everything was quiet once again.

"But...there was no one there," he said slowly, his wide eyes never leaving the door.

"Yeah, ghosts are pretty particular about who they show themselves to," Mary said.

Bradley dropped back against the counter. "But there are no such things as ghosts," he said.

"Oh, that's right, I keep forgetting," Mary said, walking across the kitchen. "You can clean up the cookie jar; I'm going to lie back down."

Chapter Thirteen

Mary woke up slowly. Every bone in her body ached and her head felt like someone had hit it with a two-by-four. "Or a log fort," she remembered.

She opened her eyes and gazed around the room. Definitely not her bedroom. Her gaze rested on Bradley sound asleep in the recliner. Most definitely not her bedroom.

She sat up slowly and eased out from under the comforter that someone, most likely Bradley, had tucked around her. She noticed the same someone had also slipped off her socks and shoes. *Okay, that was sweet. Points for him.*

She padded into the kitchen and stepped on a shard of broken cookie jar glass. "Ouch, damn, he just lost all his points."

She remembered the midnight visitor and smiled. Men were so cute when their whole belief system was whipped out from underneath them.

She opened the broom closet and swept up the small shards Bradley had missed. Then she went upstairs to examine the damage her run-in with a fort had caused.

The slightly purple and brown mark covered half of her forehead and surrounded her left eye. "I look like the Phantom of the Opera, in graphic color," she groaned. "The chief definitely gets his points back for not running away screaming."

She examined herself closer. "Obviously a man who's seen his share of hideous scenes," she muttered.

She smiled into the mirror, remembering Bradley's late night encounter with Earl. "He was so cute last night, protecting me from Earl. All *Rambo* and *X-Files* mixed together."

A knock sounded on the door.

"Mary, are you okay?" Bradley asked. "Is there someone in there with you?"

"No," Mary said, opening the door a crack and peering out. "Just talking to myself. I do that sometimes."

He looked uncomfortable, then said, "Well, you know, after last night...I didn't know if... I mean...I just wondered if some kind of, um, presence..."

He stopped and just stared.

"Bradley, did you need something?"

He closed his eyes for a moment and then sighed. "I just wanted to be sure that you were okay before I left," he said.

She stepped out and closed the bathroom door behind her.

"Ouch," Bradley grimaced. "That still looks like it hurts."

Just what a girl wants to hear, she thought.

"Oh, it looks worse than it is," she replied. "Can I make you breakfast before you leave?"

"No, I received a call and I've got to go," he said, shaking his head. "How about a rain check?"

Mary smiled. "Sure, you've got it. Thanks again for helping me last night. I really appreciate it."

"Hey, no problem," he smiled. "But before I go, I have a question."

"Sure, shoot," Mary said.

"Last night, did I dream...?"

Mary shook her head. She was not going to make this easy for him. "No, you really did break my cookie jar – but considering the circumstances, don't worry about it."

He leaned against the hallway wall, ran his hand through his hair and sighed. "Mary, did I see a ghost in your house last night?"

Mary shook her head. "No, you didn't."

He looked relieved for a moment.

"You couldn't see him. He was invisible."

"Mary, this isn't funny," he said, standing up. "I think I saw a ghost."

She leaned forward and patted his arm. "Do you want me to call your deputies and have them escort you to your office?" she asked solicitously.

"Damn it, don't be patronizing," he growled. "I don't believe in ghosts."

Mary shrugged and walked back to the bathroom. "Well, Chief, maybe they don't believe in you either," she said over her shoulder just before she closed the door. She was sure she heard a few choice words from the police chief as he stormed down her stairs.

Chapter Fourteen

A freaking ghost! He had seen a freaking ghost. Well, okay, he hadn't seen it, but he had heard it and watched it open doors. What the hell was going on in this world?

Maybe it was a trick. Maybe Mary had lured him into her house and had the whole thing set up. He rolled his eyes and shook his head. Yeah, because that was a believable scenario.

He tried to read the reports on his desk, but his eyes would blur and he would be back in her kitchen again. Watching the door open and close. Hearing the sounds of footsteps on the stairs.

Something happened in that house that he had no logical explanation for and it left him feeling unsettled.

Mayor Hank Montague, Bradley's boss, poked his head into the office. "Hey, Alden, can I talk to you?" he asked.

Bradley sat up in his chair and motioned to the seat on the other side of the desk. "Sure, Hank, what can I do for you?"

The mayor was a slight, dapper man with thick dark hair, a well-manicured moustache and piercing blue eyes. He took pride in his appearance and, Bradley thought, he considered himself quite a ladies' man.

He also had a keen intelligence and plenty of political savvy. He was able to size up a person and a situation quickly and use that knowledge to his advantage.

Bradley also noticed the mayor must have had a soft spot, because he surrounded himself with people who weren't always at the top of their game. Bradley often thought of the folks at City Hall as the island of misfit toys – people who had no other place to go. Of course, Bradley mused, it also gives the mayor a great deal of loyalty from his staff.

"So, how's the search for your wife coming along?" the mayor asked, sliding comfortably into the chair.

Bradley did a little mental head shake. Had the mayor really asked him about his wife? What the hell? That was no one's business but his, and he certainly didn't want it nosed around City Hall.

"Well, I'm not actively pursuing it right now," Bradley answered coolly.

The mayor shook his head. "Nonsense, young man," he argued. "You got the resources of the City of Freeport behind you. You go ahead and keep up with that search. You don't know if a new lead might pop out of nowhere."

Does he really think that's new advice? Bradley wondered, *or is he just trying to be helpful?*

Bradley nodded. "Thank you, sir, I'll certainly consider it."

"So your little girl, she'd be about eight now, right?" he asked. "What a tragedy, you never even saw her."

His stomach clenched. He really didn't need to be reminded that he'd never set eyes on his daughter. He didn't need to be reminded that she was almost eight years old.

"I'd really rather not discuss it, sir," Bradley said firmly.

"And your wife, she just disappeared," he continued, ignoring Bradley's wishes. "Your house broken into, your possessions taken and your wife gone. I think something like that might drive a man a little crazy."

Bradley sat up straighter. Had the mayor been doing a little digging on his own? Was this more of a threat than misguided concern? Bradley narrowed his eyes. "Is there something you need, sir?"

The mayor smiled. "Ah, yes, I almost forgot," he said. "The O'Reilly gal – the witchy one – I've been getting some calls about her. Some of the neighbors don't like the way she carries on."

"Carries on?" Bradley asked.

"You know, incantations, dancing in her back yard naked in the moonlight," the mayor paused and rubbed his chin. "'Course, I got to say I wouldn't mind watching that."

"Those would be Wiccan ceremonies," Bradley said flatly. "Ms. O'Reilly is not Wiccan. She just sees ghosts."

"Well, whatever she does and whatever she is, my constituents don't like it," he said, standing up and leaning over the desk toward Bradley. "So keep an eye on her, and if you can find some way to encourage her to move back to Chicago, I would appreciate it."

Bradley understood politics; he also understood that if he stood up, he would be taller than the mayor and that would not please him one bit. So he sat back and met the man's eyes.

"Are you asking me to harass an honest citizen of Freeport?"

The mayor chuckled. "No. No, of course not, Chief. I would never do something like that. I'm just asking you to keep an eye on a troubled gal," he smiled ingratiatingly. "We have to keep the citizens of our good city happy, or we might find ourselves without employment. You understand what I'm saying, don't you, Chief?"

Bradley just nodded, he was afraid if he opened his mouth he would lose his job.

The mayor nodded, an amused smiled playing on his lips. "Have a good day, Chief," he said as he let himself out of the office and closed the door firmly behind him.

Bradley stared at the closed door for a few moments. What the hell had he gotten himself into?

Chapter Fifteen

Two hours and a heavy make-up job later, Mary sat in her office researching the disappearance of young girls near northwest Illinois in the mid-eighties. The FBI's missing persons database provided her with the information she needed. There had been five of them, including Jessica, and none of the cases had been solved. They came from small towns within a thirty mile radius of Elizabeth – two from Illinois, two from Wisconsin and one from Iowa.

She printed out each case, four of them looked alike – they could have been sisters. Only Jessica stood out. Only Jessica was not among the ghosts that the paramedic had seen.

Mary glanced at the clock on the computer screen. It was after nine – she was sure her old pal Gracie, the shrink, was at her desk at the district office in Chicago. She dialed the number and within two rings Gracie had answered the phone.

"District 43, Gracie Williams speaking. What can I do for you?"

"Hi, Gracie, this is Mary O'Reilly. How are you doing?"

"Why Mary O'Reilly! What have you been doing with your skinny self lately? I haven't seen you laying on one of my couches for months. You still seeing ghosts?"

Mary laughed. "Yeah, I'm still seeing them and I'm still nuts. But I'm getting used to the idea…you know, psychiatric adaptation."

Gracie laughed deeply. "Girl, if you're nuts, then we'd all be better off being nuts just like you. What can I do for you, sugar? You got yourself a man you need me to analyze?"

An unbidden image of Bradley Alden flashed in Mary's mind and she pushed that thought away.

"No, no men. I'm working on a case that's about twenty-four years old. It involves at least four little girls – all about the age of eight – and perhaps another one, but I'm not sure she is part of the same case."

"What's your hunch?" Gracie asked.

"They're connected," Mary said. "I know that the girls were murdered and all brought to one place, but I don't know if they were sexually assaulted," she added.

"Well, sugar, there are a couple of choices in your cast of characters," Gracie said. "Because of the systematic way the predator has killed his victims, some good possibilities would be a child molester who was a sadistic pedophile or sociopath, or a serial killer who just happens to like eight-year-old girls."

"Okay, do you mind giving me an overview of each one, so I know what I'm looking for?" Mary asked.

"A sadistic pedophile gets a kick out of abusing their victims – sex is power and control. These are the pedophiles that kill their victims. These types search for the perfect victim and they don't mind traveling a long distance to gain access to their quarry. Think of a cougar and a hunting territory – that's your pedophile."

"Sounds like an intelligent predator," Mary said, "someone who thinks things through – not an impulse kind of guy."

"Yes, usually, this type of pedophile is intelligent and middle- to upper-class," Gracie answered. "Some of them tend to have large egos and feel that they are unstoppable. That's generally when they get caught. They act impulsively, change their patterns and make a mistake."

"So the last girl, Jessica, she might have been an impulse, rather than a planned victim?" Mary asked.

"Well, if she didn't fit his usual pattern, you could be right. He could have acted on impulse – which was more seductive because it was risky. Which could have caused him to change some other part of his modus operandi," she replied. "Also, if she was an impulse, it was likely an impulse opportunity – so look for your molester to have closer ties to that community than the other ones he was hunting in.

"But she could have stumbled on him killing one of the other girls," she added, "and just got in the way. You gotta cover all your angles."

"Okay, how about the other kind of child molester?" Mary asked.

"A sociopath uses violence to have power over others – sexual violence is not sex gone too far, it is violence with sex as its instrument," Gracie explained. "And once again you have someone who has a big ego and loves power."

"Like a politician," Mary mused.

Gracie laughed. "Girl, I like my job – I take the Fifth!"

"All right, how about a serial killer?" Mary asked.

"You're going to see a lot of similarities here, sugar. A serial killer is a person who murders three or more people over a period of more than thirty days, with a 'cooling off' period between each murder," Gracie said. "The motivation for killing is largely based on psychological gratification. But often a sexual element is involved with the killings. The murders may have been attempted or completed in a similar fashion and the victims may have had something in common."

"Okay, according to the FBI files – after that final missing girl, I haven't been able to find any other missing children matching that description," Mary said. "Does that mean he's stopped?"

"No, it could mean a number of things," Gracie answered. "Could be he's in jail, arrested for something totally different. Could be he's dead. Could be he's sick or injured and can't physically continue to prey on his victims. Could be that he moved away.

"Then again," she continued, "it could be that the last one scared him and he got more careful. He's probably still finding ways to feed his hunger – maybe pornography or abusive sex with an adult partner, or he might have gotten better at hiding his crimes – but he's still out there. Sugar, be careful, from what you've said, this predator is smart and skillful. And even twenty-four years later, he's paranoid and is looking over his shoulder. If you trap that cougar, you make sure you got the means to put him down."

Mary shivered. Her gut told her that he was still out there.

"Thanks, Gracie, this helps a lot," Mary said.

"Oh, anytime," Gracie replied. "If you send me those cases, I'll see if I just can't put together a more detailed report for you – on my break time."

Mary chuckled. "Thanks, I owe you."

"Honey, I'll remember that, and when I need a ghostbuster, you'd best be on my doorstep in record time."

Mary laughed. "I'll break all kinds of speeding records."

"Just don't get caught!"

Chapter Sixteen

Mary zipped off an email to Gracie with the case files attached and then reviewed her notes from her interview with Lisa. She would be meeting with the Ryersons in an hour and she wanted to be sure she had her facts straight.

She was packing her information into her briefcase when Rosie burst into her office.

"What did you do to your face?" Rosie asked.

Mary's hand went up to her cheek. "I thought I had covered it up pretty well," Mary replied. "You think it still looks bad?"

Rosie stopped in front of Mary and peered closely at her face. "Well, if someone didn't know you…" she began.

"So, if they thought I was born this way, they wouldn't notice," Mary said. "Thanks."

"Well, the idea behind make-up is to blend, not scoop it on like frosting," Rosie replied. "What happened?"

Mary shrugged. "No, big deal, I ran into the fort at Apple River."

"Well, of course you did," she said, examining Mary's face again. "Go to the bathroom and wash your face."

"But…"

"No arguments," she said, "wash."

When Mary returned, Rosie was just re-entering the office with a large box in her hands.

"What's that?" Mary asked.

"My emergency kit," Rosie said.

She placed the box on the desk and lifted the lid. Inside were smaller boxes of assorted make-up, hairspray, nail polish, some cartons of nylons and a collection of scarves.

"What kind of emergencies?" Mary asked.

"Fashion emergencies," Rosie responded. "You should always be prepared."

In the bottom of the box Mary saw what she thought was a flesh-colored beach ball. She pulled it out and realized that it was a life-sized blow-up woman.

"What in the world?" Mary asked.

"My third husband bought that," Rosie said. "Not for that!" she exclaimed at Mary's shocked face. "We used it for the boutique I owned. It was a portable mannequin. Now I find that it's handy for seeing if outfits work."

"You try your clothes on a dress up doll?" Mary teased.

Rosie didn't seem embarrassed at all.

"One can never be lax in preparing one's outward appearance," Rosie admonished. "You are judged by how you present yourself. Now sit."

Mary obediently sat at her desk while Rosie applied makeup using a little white piece of foam to the tender area around Mary's eye. "Ouch," Mary said.

"Don't whine," Rosie said. "Beauty hurts."

The door opened again and Stanley joined them. He walked over to Mary and winked.

"So, Mary, the word on the street is that the police chief's car was parked in front of your house all night," Stanley teased, and then he really looked at her. "What did you do to your face, girlie?"

"That's right," Rosie added. "I heard that too, that's why I came over in the first place. She ran into a fort, Stanley," she added.

"Well of course she did," Stanley said without a pause. "Now about that police chief."

"When the police chief saw how I looked last night, he had the same reaction as you two. But the bruise was fresher and obviously more colorful at the time," she explained. "And I was not very steady on my feet.

"He helped me into my house and I passed out on the couch soon after," she continued. "So he stayed on the recliner all night – just watching out for me. It was nice."

"Wonder if he'd do the same for me?" Stanley smirked and elbowed Rosie. "Oh, Police Chief, I do believe I have a headache," Stanley said in a high falsetto.

"Well, if you talked to him like that, he'd probably arrest you for solicitation," Mary said dryly.

Rosie giggled. "Besides, a bruise like this could only improve your looks, Stanley."

"Ha, ha, very funny," he replied, sneering at Rosie. "So, how come all of the sudden you're not a nut case?"

Mary chuckled. "Well, I was probably still in the 'nut case' category when he helped me into the house. But by the time he left this morning, I think he was reconsidering his own sanity."

"What happened?" Rosie asked, standing back a little to see how Mary's face looked.

"He met Earl," she laughed.

"You mean, headless dead-guy Earl?" Rosie asked.

"Well, he didn't actually see Earl," Mary corrected, and then in a Boris Karloff accent added, "He heard Earl and saw the door open and close by itself."

Stanley chuckled and sat down on the edge of the desk. "Well, poor Police Chief Alden, that must've scared the crap out of him."

"He actually handled it very well," Mary said, "once he put his gun away. The only casualty was my cookie jar."

"Well, I never liked that cookie jar anyway," Rosie said, turning Mary's head to each side. "Mary, I think I've done it."

"Thanks, Rosie," Mary said, "I really try to avoid scaring clients."

Mary turned to Stanley. "Okay, so how do you think I look?" she asked.

"Can't hardly see the bruise," Stanley agreed.

"Well, good," Mary said, standing up and grabbing her purse. "Hey, lock up for me – okay?"

She gave Rosie a hug. "Thanks again, I appreciate it."

She started to walk out the door, but stopped and turned back to Stanley. "No teasing the chief about Earl. Promise?"

Stanley sighed. "Yeah, I suppose. Spoilsport."

Mary grinned. "You don't want me to end up in the hoosegow again – do you?"

Stanley chuckled. "Get out of here."

Chapter Seventeen

An hour later, Mary pulled up to the front of the Ryerson home and parked her car. Her first instinct was to meet with the senator alone, to not only spare Susan from the information about Renee's pregnancy, but to also gauge his reaction without his wife in the room. Unfortunately, she was not offered that choice.

"We'll meet with you together, Miss O'Reilly," Senator Joseph Ryerson said, as he guided her to the parlor where she had met with Susan during their last meeting at their home. "I have nothing to hide from my wife. We have no secrets."

Ryerson was tall and handsome. Even though his thick brown hair now had gray highlights, Mary could still see the boyish good looks that would have attracted Renee twenty-four years ago. She could also see intelligence in his eyes; this was not a man who was easily fooled. She'd have to see if he was as honest as he was intelligent.

Mary watched him slide his arm comfortably around his wife as they sat on the couch together.

Very smooth, she thought, *but it'll take more than that to convince me.*

She smiled politely and took the offered cup of tea. Then she leaned forward in her chair and waited until the right moment.

The senator had lifted his cup nearly to his mouth when she asked, "Were you aware that Renee Peterson was carrying your child when she was murdered?"

The fine bone china slipped from his hand, crashed against the coffee table and broke. The senator's face was pale and he was visibly shaken.

Well, if that's acting, he's good, Mary thought.

Susan Ryerson had been able to lower her cup to the saucer, although her hand shook. She sat still for a few moments and then belatedly placed her hand on top of her husband's. He automatically turned his hand over and squeezed. Susan's hand stayed woodenly motionless.

"How did you...?" he paused for a moment, closing his eyes. When he spoke, his voice was slightly hoarse. "Are you sure?"

Mary nodded. "Yes, I'm sure."

"Did she get the chance to share that news with you, Senator?" Mary questioned.

He shook his head. "No. No. I never knew..."

"Mrs. Ryerson, did you by chance know of Renee's pregnancy?"

Susan pulled her hand away from her husband's and clasped them together tightly. Her eyes narrowed and she said, "Do you think I would have hired you if I had known?"

No, she wouldn't have hired me, Mary thought. *She would not have been willing to expose her husband's position, their position, to public scandal.*

Susan turned to her husband. "How could you have been so stupid? She was only a child herself."

Joseph shook his head and turned to his wife. "I was foolish. I was careless. And I was enamored with the idea that a cute, young woman would be attracted to me."

Then he turned to Mary. "But I didn't know about the..." He paused. "...the baby. We were supposed to meet that night, but when I got there she was floating on top of the pool."

"Susan, you never answered my question. Did you know about the pregnancy?" Mary said. "I need you to answer me."

"No, I did not know that Renee Peterson was pregnant," she said. "Although, as I mentioned to you earlier, I did suspect that my husband was having an affair with her."

Joseph looked surprised. "You knew?" he asked.

She shook her head. "I was your wife, didn't you think I'd know?" she replied.

The senator looked down at the floor for a few moments. He lifted his head and sought his wife's eyes. "I was so stupid," he said. "Thank you for staying with me."

She hesitantly smiled back at him. "Well, you've made it worth it."

He reached over, took her hand and enveloped it in both of his. This time, the clasp was returned.

"I love you, you know."

Susan smiled, her eyes tearing slightly. "Yes, I know."

Mary knew politicians were used to being in the public eye. She also knew politicians were used to putting up a good façade in the midst of turmoil. Could she believe the emotion she had just witnessed, or was it merely for her benefit?

"Senator, Susan, was there anyone else who might have spoken with Renee that evening?" she asked. "Anyone who might have learned her secret and thought she was a liability to your political future?"

"Renee didn't confide in the other members of my staff because she didn't want to accidentally expose our relationship," Joseph said. "She didn't want to jeopardize my campaign.

"Besides," he added, "I don't believe that anyone on my staff would have the ability to commit murder. They are all good people."

"Well, begging your pardon, Senator," Mary said, "but one of those good people, either someone from your staff or one of your supporters, did murder Renee Peterson on the night of your party."

Joseph was taken aback for a moment. He nodded. "You're right, of course, it's just hard to believe."

"Can you tell me anything about Renee before she came to work for you?" Mary asked. "Anything about her family life or her previous work experience?"

An hour later Mary had more data, but she knew she was no closer to finding Renee's murderer than she was that morning. She hadn't ruled out the senator, he had plenty of motive, especially if he had, indeed, known about the pregnancy. She hadn't ruled out Susan either – she could have worked with her husband to murder Renee in order to clear the way for their political careers. No one was in the clear yet and Mary was not going to stop until she found out who killed Renee Peterson.

Chapter Eighteen

Mary wondered if the Freeport Republic had issued a restraining order against her, but she figured that if she hadn't seen it, it didn't exist. Ignorance is bliss. She took a deep breath and strolled through the newsroom with false bravado, tapped on Jerry's glass wall and walked in.

"Hi, Jerry," she said, making herself comfortable in the chair in front of his desk.

"What'cha want, O'Reilly?" he growled, his head studying the computer screen. "I'm on deadline."

Mary smiled. That was Jerry's usual greeting, so perhaps he didn't know about the warrant.

"I need to talk to you about Renee Peterson," she said, scooting the chair forward. Jerry didn't budge.

"Never heard of her," was his curt reply.

"Aw, come on, Jerry," Mary said, "you worked with her on Senator Ryerson's campaign. Remember?"

Jerry looked up from the screen and at Mary.

"The gal who drowned?" he asked. "Little Renee?"

Mary nodded. "Yeah, that's the one."

"Sure, I remember her. Cute gal. She was from around here wasn't she?" Jerry said, leaning back in his chair. "I always thought she had a crush on the senator. Too bad about the drowning."

"So, do you think that she and the senator...?" Mary asked, lifting one eyebrow suggestively. "You know...?"

"Are you kidding?" Jerry asked. "Have you seen the doll he's married to? No, didn't happen. Besides, he wasn't that kind of guy."

So much for reporter's intuition, Mary thought.

"So, what was your job during the campaign?" Mary asked.

"Why are you asking so many questions?" Jerry asked, his beefy hands placed flat on his desk as he leaned toward her. "Is there some sleazy rag paying you money to dig something up on the senator just before he goes for the big run?"

"More like someone is paying me to make sure there's nothing to dig up," she said.

"Oh, so you're one of the good guys?"

Mary smiled. "Always, Jerry. Always."

"Okay, well, then I'll answer your question," Jerry replied, sitting back in his chair. "I did all of the media stuff – press releases, setting up press conferences, schmoozing with the reporters – that kind of stuff."

"So, did you go to all of his press conferences?"

Jerry shook his head. "No, I just set them up," he said. "The senator could handle the press when he was on the road. Besides, someone needed to handle stuff at headquarters in case something came up."

"Do you remember the night Renee died?" Mary asked.

Jerry paused for a moment, remembering back. "Yeah, I remember, although, I was a little buzzed," he laughed regretfully. "Some people celebrate with champagne. For me…"

He mimicked taking a drag and smiled. "It was my relaxant of choice."

Mary could not picture Jerry – slightly obese, fiftyish and balding – as a stoner. She shook her head to get rid of the mental image.

"Okay, so you were flying a little," Mary said. "What do you remember?"

"I remember the senator's speech," he said. "I remember Renee, Mike and me standing at the back of the ballroom, near the patio doors, giving the senator the thumbs up on his speech.

"Then Renee says she's gonna take a walk," he said, shaking his head. "You know, maybe if I hadn't been high, I could have saved her."

"So Renee goes outside," Mary prompted.

"Yeah, and I follow her out," Jerry said. "We talk for a minute on the patio and then she walks out by the gardens and I go the other way, behind the garage to celebrate a little more."

"Did anyone celebrate with you?" Mary asked.

"No, I kept that stuff to myself," he said. "I didn't want it to reflect badly on the senator."

"How long were you away from the party?"

Jerry shrugged. "The next thing I remember is the senator running through the gardens, he's got Renee in his arms and he's yelling for an ambulance.

"A real shame," he added. "She was such a nice girl."

"Sounds like she was. Thanks, Jerry," Mary said, "this is going to help."

"Hey, anytime," he said cordially.

Just then, a reporter walked past his office and his smile became the usual growl. "Yeah, O'Reilly, next time remember that some of us have deadlines," he yelled. "Next time make an appointment."

Mary smiled and winked. "Yes, sir, I'll remember. I promise."

Jerry looked around first, and when the coast was clear winked back.

Chapter Nineteen

He felt like a stalker. There was no reason for him to be sitting in his cruiser outside Mary's house. No reason except a thinly veiled threat from his boss.

Bradley wondered how much digging the mayor had done and who he had spoken to. He knew that his old boss would not have offered anything but praise for the work Bradley had done while he worked for him. But that had been seven years ago and during the last year Bradley had worked on the force, he had taken so many personal days, he might as well have been AWOL.

He could recall that summer day over eight years ago with perfect clarity. He was driving his patrol unit on his usual route when the call came in. Forced entry. Shots fired. He was on alert immediately, but when dispatch listed his address, he was like a man possessed.

All of those years of training had him automatically calling in to the operator, letting her know that he was responding to the crime scene. He didn't even remember driving to his house. He only remembered pulling up to the curb and dashing from his unit through the open front door.

His chief had beat him to the scene and had to physically restrain him in the front hall. "You go rushing through there, messing things up, you ain't helping no one," he had whispered harshly. "Now, you tell me when you got yourself together and then we can proceed."

It took Bradley only a few moments to gain control. "Where's Jeannine?" he asked.

The chief shook his head. "She ain't here," he said. "We got an APB out on her already. No blood. No specific sign of struggle, but the place has been tossed."

Bradley looked around. Really looked for the first time. It was as if a tornado had ripped through the inside of his house. Furniture was upturned, pictures were off the walls, books and knickknacks strewn across the room and drawers pulled out and dumped.

"You working undercover on anything right now?" his chief asked. "Someone mad at you?"

Bradley shook his head. "Nothing. Nothing that I can think of."

"Yeah, well, you probably ain't thinking too straight right now anyway," his chief said. "Give us a minute, then I'll have one of the guys walk you through the house and you can tell us if anything's missing."

"Other than my wife," Bradley said through clenched teeth.

The chief nodded. "Yeah, other than Jeannine."

Bradley couldn't believe she was gone. She had to be in the house. She had to be fine. This had to be a big mistake. They just weren't looking in the right places.

"Chief, I can't stand here," he said. "I've got to…"

"Williams," the chief called to another officer. "I want you to let Alden search through the house. Give him any assistance he needs."

Bradley nodded to the chief. "Thanks."

Each room was more damaged than the last. Whoever had done this to his house went about it in a systematic and purely destructive manner. He checked all of the places he thought she might have hidden – closets, crawl spaces, attic and even the garage and the shed. There was no sign of his wife. Then he went back and checked them all a second time.

"Alden, come here," the chief had called when Bradley was going back a third time. "I gotta talk to you for a moment."

Fearing the worst, Bradley rushed to his side. "Have you heard…?"

The chief shook his head. "No, no, nothing like that," he said. "I got a question for you. You and Jeannine, was everything, you know, okay between the two of you?"

Bradley was astonished. "You think that I…"

"No, no," the chief stopped him at once. "You know, sometimes wives get tired of being married to the job. You know. Could Jeannine have just decided that it was time for her to just disappear? Could she have done this?"

He immediately remembered just a week prior looking at the monitor at the doctor's office, watching the baby that was growing inside Jeannine. She was beaming as she lovingly stroked her expanding belly. "She's gorgeous," she'd whispered tearfully.

He had leaned over and placed a kiss on her forehead. "Looks just like her mom," he had said softly, awed by the image on the screen. "She's so active."

Jeannine had laughed. "Yeah, just wait until she's two."

Overcome with joy, he'd felt like he was going to burst.

Bradley shook his head. "No. No way," he said firmly. "She is, we both are, excited about the baby. We found out last week we're having a girl. Jeannine bought pink paint. I'm supposed to paint the nursery this weekend. No, no way did she leave me."

In the months and years that followed, Bradley wondered about his answer time and time again. Was he wrong? Was she tired of him? Was there another man? Was she living somewhere else, raising their daughter with another man?

The chief allowed him to participate in the investigation. But after a year, when all of the leads had dried up, Bradley had taken a leave of absence and followed up every insignificant piece of data. He traveled all across the country, checking morgues and hospitals for any pregnant Jane Does, searching vital statistic records for baby girls born at the time that his daughter would have been born, reading newspapers, interviewing other police forces, and spending hours online looking for something, anything that could help him find his wife and his daughter.

Eighteen months ago, he finally stopped and took a good look at his life. He had lost his home, his savings, his job, his friends and very nearly lost his mind. And he was no closer to solving the mystery than he had been six and a half years ago. One thing he knew for sure: he needed a new start. He couldn't go back and live in the town where it all had happened.

One call to his old chief had opened doors for him; he had been interviewed and got the job as Chief of Police in Freeport.

"So now, here I am," he muttered with disgust, "stalking someone to keep the boss happy. You've come a long way, baby."

The back porch light of Mary's house clicked on. Bradley sat up straight and peered out the side window. He caught a quick glimpse of Mary leaving her house, dressed in black once again.

"Well, if nothing else, it won't be a boring night," he said as he turned the engine on and slowly drove down the street.

Chapter Twenty

Mary figured she owed Earl. Bradley hadn't bothered her all day. And he'd probably think twice before he called her a kook again. So even though she was close to exhausted, she found herself lying in bed that night dressed in her black jeans, a black turtleneck and black running shoes, with her black leather jacket thrown over the banister for easy access.

The clock struck midnight and the familiar shuffling began. Mary waited for Earl to make his way through the kitchen and up the stairs. His bloodied uniformed figure stood in the doorway of her room. Mary sat up in her bed. "Okay Lieutenant, why don't you show me what has kept you up for so long."

Earl turned and started back down the hall, with Mary following. The raw stump where his head used to be was pretty gross, so Mary turned her eyes to his feet scuffling across the carpet.

"Remember Earl, I'm not like you – so no going through walls," Mary said, as she grabbed her jacket. "Instead of the basement, maybe we could use the back door."

Earl paused and shrugged.

"Shrugs are weird when you don't have a head," Mary decided.

Earl reached the first floor and, instead of turning toward the basement, he headed to the back door. When he reached it he began to knock against it with his whole body. "Wait. Wait. WAIT!" Mary yelled, moving around Earl. "I'll open it, okay? You don't have to knock down my door."

She reached for the doorknob and found it covered with Earl's blood. "Oh, gross!" she exclaimed. "Really, did you have to do that?"

She turned the knob and pulled the door open. The cold air rushed in and brought with it a blast of Earl's rotting smell. "You know, nothing personal, but I'm going to be really glad when you're on the other side."

Earl moved slowly down the stairs, out into the backyard and then down the street. Once on the street his gait increased to a quick clip. "I can tell you were a soldier," Mary said and jogged down the street behind him, trying to stay upwind if at all possible.

An obese tabby sat on the front banister of a colonial style house, lazily watching moths flutter around a porch light. It slowly turned its head as they approached, ready to send them a disdainful cat "I'm ignoring you" look. But when it got a good look at Earl, its reaction was immediate – back arched and hair standing on end – it dove off the porch and climbed up the nearest tree.

"Sorry," Mary called. "If you're not down by morning, I'll call the fire department."

They had traveled about a mile and a half when Earl started to slow. He turned right on Carroll Street and headed for the large estate that was now the Stephenson County Historical Museum.

The Taylor House, a beautiful limestone mansion, sat in the midst of the lovingly tended arboretum. The Taylor Gardeners, a group of devoted volunteers, had dedicated hours creating the small gardens and park-like setting throughout the three acres.

Mary followed the winding driveway that led to the front of the home. Large trees bordered the drive, their bare branches illuminated against the full moon. Mary glanced toward the house and saw the familiar shadows of the former residents flit past the tall windows. This was a place filled with contented ghosts who occasionally visited a place they loved when they were still alive. Those ghosts were always a joy to encounter.

Mary glanced around and saw a sweet elderly woman kneeling in the midst of a small English garden. She was methodically pulling up weeds. Mary moved closer and the woman turned. She smiled up at Mary and faded into the night.

She noted that Earl hadn't stopped at the front, but had drifted along the south side of the house, past the sunroom. Mary hurried forward, careful not to do anything that would trigger an alarm; she didn't need another incident with the police department. She bypassed the kitchen entrance to the house and continued to the back of the property.

In one corner, far behind the mansion was a modern carriage-house that accommodated the Museum Director's office and meeting rooms. Adjacent to the little house was an ancient ornamental wrought-iron fence that housed the family cemetery.

Earl stopped at the wrought-iron gate and motioned to Mary. She opened the gate for him, he glided through and stopped. He paused for a moment and waited for Mary to join him. "Almost there, Earl, we're almost at the end of the journey."

He moved to the northwest corner of the graveyard, turned back to Mary and pointed. The limestone grave marker was nearly worn smooth. Mary knelt next to it and took out her penlight. She shone it against the engraving. UNKNOWN UNION SOLDIER – APRIL 1864.

That made sense. The Taylors often hosted Union Soldiers before they left for war. It was just like them to honor the death of an unknown soldier.

Mary took out an index card that she had prepared that evening, it read, "Lieutenant Earl Belvidere." She taped it to the headstone and looked up at Earl. "That's the best I can do for now," she explained. "As soon as I get the other information, I'll get you a new stone. You won't be unknown anymore."

Earl straightened, turned to Mary, saluted her and slowly faded into the darkness of the night. Mary rubbed a hand over the headstone and her eyes filled with tears. "Goodbye Earl, happy travels."

"So, Earl won't be breaking into your house anymore?"

Mary nearly screamed. "You scared the hell out of me!"

Bradley chuckled and stooped down next to her. "I didn't think anything scared you," he said.

"Very funny," Mary replied, wiping the remaining tears from her eyes. "How long have you been following me?"

Bradley shrugged. "Since you left your house."

"My house," she paused for a moment. "Am I under surveillance?"

He shook his head, guilt weighing heavy on his conscience. "No, of course not, but the bomb incident has left me feeling a little uneasy."

"Bradley, I swear, I didn't plant a bomb," she said.

He stood and then offered his hand to help her up. "I don't think you did," he explained. "But someone did. So that means that someone is trying to frame you. Why?"

"Maybe it was just a mistake," she said, brushing the dried leaves and dirt from the knees of her jeans. "Maybe someone else planted a bomb – like one of the authors of the crazy letters to the editor. But because someone saw me there earlier, they thought it was me. A simple matter of mistaken identity."

"I don't buy it," he said.

He guided her to where his cruiser was parked.

"Where are you taking me?" she asked.

He grinned. "Well, first we've got to get that poor cat out of the tree and then I'll take you home."

Mary smiled. "Thanks. Earl really freaked that poor kitty out."

"I sympathize with the cat," Bradley said.

She laughed as she settled into the seat and strapped on her seat belt. "And this is much better than walking back home."

"Yeah, this way I can keep a closer eye on you," Bradley said, feeling another twinge of guilt at his choice of words.

They drove through the darkened streets and parked down the block from the house with its cat in a tree.

"I don't want to draw too much attention to us," Bradley said, as they exited the vehicle.

"Yeah, because a woman all dressed in black and a policeman in uniform standing outside a house and calling, 'Kitty, kitty, kitty,' isn't going to draw any attention at all," Mary replied.

"Mary."

"Yes?"

"Shut up."

Mary giggled. "Yes, sir."

The poor cat was right where Mary had left it earlier, clinging to a branch about ten feet in the air.

"Awww, poor kitty," Mary crooned. "Come on down. The big, bad ghost is all gone now."

The cat looked down at Mary and meowed piteously, but didn't budge.

"Kitty, kitty, kitty," Bradley called.

"Did you know that your voice raises at least an octave when you do that?" Mary asked. "It's almost disturbing."

"Mary."

Mary chuckled. "Yeah, I know. Shut up."

Bradley moved closer to the tree and reached up toward the branches. "Come on, kitty," he pleaded. "Come on down."

Mary moved next to him. "Here kitty, kitty, kitty."

The front door of the house burst open. A heavy-set middle-aged man with a terry-cloth robe barely covering his ratty tee-shirt and boxers exited with a shotgun in his hands.

"Hey, you, whaddya doing in my front yard?"

Bradley moved away from the tree into the light shining from the front porch. "I apologize, we were on patrol and noticed your cat in the tree," he said. "We were just trying to get her down."

The man peered into the darkness toward Mary. "You and who else? Cat woman?" he asked.

Mary swallowed a giggle and stayed where she was, under the tree.

"No, an undercover law enforcement officer," Bradley improvised, "helping the department with some specialty training."

"And you stopped to get a cat out of a tree?" he put the shotgun down and scratched his head. "Is that how my tax dollars are being spent? What kind of specialty training?"

"Night ops," Bradley said.

"Night ops my ass," the man replied. "Horace, get down from that tree right now and get your butt inside."

The cat scrambled down the tree and dashed through the open door. "Now can I get some sleep?" he demanded.

"Yes, sir, have a good evening, sir," Bradley said.

"Bunch of kooks, middle of the night, night ops," the man muttered as he closed his door.

Mary doubled over in laughter as Bradley stormed past her toward the cruiser. "People used to have respect for the law," he said.

"Obviously the man doesn't appreciate the danger associated with the job," she giggled. "You could have received some really deep scratches."

Bradley continued toward the cruiser, trying to ignore her.

"Wait, dear, don't forget cat woman," she called, tears beginning to stream down her face. Bradley turned back. Mary could see him struggling not to laugh.

"Night ops my ass," she mocked and bent over to catch her breath.

The bullet whizzed past her and exploded into the tree bark above her. Her laughter stopped immediately. She dropped to the ground only seconds before Bradley dropped next to her, his gun drawn, his eyes very serious.

"Which way did it come from?" he asked.

"Across the street, northwest," Mary stuttered, her body shaking in reaction to the close call.

"Hey, are you okay?" Bradley asked, sliding closer.

"Last time I got shot, I died," she replied, taking a deep shuddering breath. "Just give me a minute and I'll be okay."

"Shit!" he swore. "Hang in there. I'm going to call for reinforcements."

He pulled his radio from his holster. "This is Alden, I'm on Demeter near LaCresta, shots fired. I need back-up immediately."

"So," he said, putting his arm around Mary and pulling her alongside him. "I've never met someone who died. I mean someone who could actually talk to me about it. Was it all bright lights and Mormon Tabernacle Choir music?"

She smiled in spite of her fear. She'd used this tactic before with victims in their first stages of shock to calm them down until help could get there. "Well, I can't really be sure but I think I remember hearing Queen's 'Another One Bites The Dust,'" she quipped.

He snorted. "Well, at least it wasn't ACDC's 'Highway to Hell.'"

She chuckled, and although it was comforting to have him next to her, shielding her, she knew that she needed to figure out what was going on. "So, who do you think is trying to kill me?" she asked.

"Hey, it could have been me they were after," he replied.

"No," she turned her head and looked at him. "We both know that bullet had my name on it."

He turned back, his face grim, his lips set tightly. "Mary..."

The approaching sounds of sirens halted their conversation for the moment.

"That was fast," she said.

"They're good guys," he replied. "I know they have my back."

Mary slowly did an examination of the area around her, looking at all of the places people could conceal themselves. Suddenly the safe residential street she had just jogged through with Earl had changed from a quiet garden to a dangerous jungle. "Do you think he's still out there?" Mary asked.

"Not if he's smart," Bradley answered. "If he's smart, he hightailed it as soon as he got that first shot off."

"So I've been laying on this cold ground next to you for nothing?" she teased.

"Hey, I thought it was a bonding moment." He smiled at her.

She grinned back. Three Freeport Police Department cruisers pulled up to the curb in front of them and three uniformed cops, their guns drawn, exited the vehicles.

"Chief, are you okay?" one of the officers asked.

"Yes, thanks for getting here so quickly," Bradley responded.

"I think we can get up now," Bradley added, standing and offering Mary his hand.

"Thanks for your help," she said to the officers.

"No problem, ma'am," one of the younger officers replied.

"Well, I still owe you a ride home," Bradley said.

"That would be really nice," she said.

"And I'm going to station one of these nice officers outside your house tonight," he continued, "just in case."

"You know I'm licensed to carry," she said. "I can protect myself."

"Yeah, I figured," he said. "Just the same, I'd feel better knowing someone was out there. Just one favor."

"Sure. What?"

"Don't shoot my officer."

"Bradley."

"What?"

"Shut up."

Chapter Twenty-one

Mary sat in the City Council Chamber watching the circus that was going on around her. Mayor Hank Montague had decided that the "shooting incident" as he called it, needed to be reported to the press so that the good citizens of Freeport could be aware.

She watched the press representatives from the Freeport Republic, the local radio station and the television stations from Rockford, the nearest major city, jockey for position in the small chamber room.

Mary turned to see the mayor speaking with Bradley in the corner of the room. Although he stood about a head shorter than Bradley, his open smile, animated movements and friendly manner drew your eye. *He is*, Mary thought, *the ultimate politician.*

She could see how he would have been an asset in Senator Ryerson's campaign.

Mary met him when she first opened her business. He stopped by to welcome her to the area. Once she had told him what she did – paranormal investigation – he seemed to give her a little distance. Mary shrugged. Of course, many people get freaked when you mention ghosts.

Mary tapped her fingers against the arm of the chair. This was ridiculous. The public did not need to be aware that someone was using her for target practice. *Well actually,* she amended mentally, *we're spinning the story to make it look like some crackpot is taking shots at the Chief of Police.*

Both Mary and Bradley decided that was the best way to handle it.

"So, you and Miss O'Reilly were out together in your cruiser for what reason?" the reporter from The Freeport Republic asked Bradley.

Mary played the truthful scenario through in her mind.

Well, Miss O'Reilly was following a ghost that was about one-hundred-fifty years old through the streets in order to make sure his remains were identified and he could rest in peace instead of walking through our streets and frightening defenseless cats.

Nope, that isn't going to work, she decided.

"As most of you know, Miss O'Reilly is a decorated former Chicago police officer," she heard Bradley say.

She didn't think he'd remember that.

"She's received many commendations, especially in the area of gang relations and vice," he continued.

She knew she hadn't told him that.

"Her experience is invaluable and the police department appreciates her willingness to share that knowledge with us," Bradley said. "Miss O'Reilly was pointing out areas of potential risks in the city last night."

"You feel that Demeter and LaCresta is an area of high risk?" the reporter asked. Demeter and LaCresta was one of the quietest areas in the city.

"No," Bradley stated. "As Mr. Walker mentioned during his part of the interview, we happened to see that his cat, Horace, was up a tree, and we stopped to assist it."

Mary turned to look at Mr. Walker, who looked much better fully dressed. He thanked them profusely, convinced that the "thugs" that shot at Mary were actually after Horace.

"Damned right," Mr. Walker interrupted. "They probably saved Horace's life."

He turned menacingly toward the reporter.

"You got a problem with that?"

The young reporter shook his head. "No, no sir, I'm glad that Horace is safe."

The reporter turned to Mary. "Miss O'Reilly, I can't help but notice that your face is bruised, did that occur during the altercation last night?"

No, I ran into a fort a day earlier, she thought. *Nope, that wasn't going to work either.*

"No, it didn't," she said out loud. "Thanks to the quick reflexes of Chief Alden, I was in a secure position moments after the shot was fired."

"Where did you receive the injury?" the reporter asked. "I understand the chief's vehicle was outside your house for most of the night, the evening before this incident."

Why you little gossip, she silently accused.

"Because I am a private investigator, I can't divulge any specifics. However, I did receive fairly serious head-trauma during an altercation related to a case I am working on," she said. "The chief received this information through proper channels and because we didn't want to put any local health care facility under duress, he agreed to monitor my condition. Not only do I, but also the agencies that I am currently contracting with, appreciate his help in this matter."

Okay, maybe I'm laying it on a little thick, she thought, *but damn it, he's just looking for dirt.*

The reporter's eyes widened. "Agencies?" he repeated. "Would those be federal agencies?"

Well, Apple River Fort is listed on the National Register of Historic Places, so that's a federal agency, she added silently.

"As I said earlier, I really can't give you specifics," she said. "But yes, a federal agency was involved."

"Thank you, Miss O'Reilly," he said, with a little more respect in his voice.

"Mayor Montague, do you have any comments about what happened last night in Freeport?" the reporter asked.

"First, I want to express my gratitude that both Miss O'Reilly and Police Chief Alden survived this ordeal without any serious consequences," he said. "And I appreciate the quick acting response of Freeport's Police Department coming to the aid of the police chief. This is an example of the wonderful public servants we have in this town."

Wonderful public servants brought to you by Mayor Montague. Is there any politician that doesn't make every positive incident all about them, Mary wondered?

After the press conference, Hank Montague approached Mary and Bradley.

"Good job last night," he said. "It's good to know that the only casualty was an oak tree."

"And from what I understand, Mayor, it was only a flesh wound," Mary replied lightly.

The mayor turned and smiled at her. "I'd hate to see a flesh wound on skin as pretty as yours, young lady," he said, stroking his hand intimately along her cheek. "You need to take care."

"Yes, sir, I will. Thank you," Mary said, stepping out of the reach of his touch.

"See that you do," the mayor replied, his eyes narrowing slightly.

"We'll be examining that bullet to see if we can trace it back to the weapon involved," Bradley said, drawing the mayor's attention to him.

"Excellent," the mayor said, slapping Bradley on the back. "Excellent job, young man."

An hour later Mary and Bradley were sitting in his office, eating sandwiches and arguing.

"You do understand what a confidentiality agreement is, don't you?" Mary asked.

"You do understand what being shot is, don't you?" Bradley replied. "You already died once. I don't think that makes you invincible, does it?"

Mary winced and then shook her head. "No, but having done it once, I can tell you that I don't want to experience it again anytime soon. So I am careful."

"Running into a fort is being careful?"

"Bradley, you obviously don't understand, so let me explain this to you. When a ghost needs to show me what happened to them, so I can investigate their circumstances, I'm kind of transported back to their time," she said. "Everything looks like it was when whatever happened took place."

"Yes, and when you are wandering around in the 1980s you are completely defenseless," Bradley countered.

"Now that I know that someone is out to get me, I'll be more aware," she said. "I won't put myself in a situation that might compromise my safety."

"So you can control when you transport back?" he asked.

She took a bite of her pickle spear to prolong the moment before she had to answer. "Well, actually, before this case, I never transported before," she admitted. "And so far, it hasn't been planned."

"What makes this case so different?" he asked.

"Probably murder," she replied.

"Murder?" Bradley asked, dropping his sandwich onto his plate. "This case involves murder?"

Chapter Twenty-two

"Well, that went well," Mary muttered sarcastically as she jogged down the steps of the police station and headed up Main Street toward her office. Logically she could understand Bradley's concern. Growing up with a house full of men, she also understood the alpha-male need to protect others. But damn it, she was a former Chicago cop. Did he really think that she couldn't handle her own investigation?

She looked down the street at the patrol car slowly following her. Obviously not.

She entered her office and watched the patrol car glide down the street and park halfway up the block. The officer was positioned so he could watch the door of her office and her car.

"This is a total waste of taxpayer money," Mary muttered. "I'm going to write my congressman."

Instead, she picked up the phone and called Rosie. "Hi, Rosie. Can you and Stanley come down to my office? I need your help. Oh, and bring your emergency box."

Rosie and Stanley arrived within fifteen minutes.

"So, I see you're being staked out," Stanley said as he entered. "You've been planting more bombs lately?"

Mary grinned. "No, the police chief wasn't thrilled that I didn't see fit to share my case with him," she said with a shrug. "So I'm being tailed."

"How exciting," Rosie trilled. "Do you want us to create a diversion while you speed away?"

"Well, speeding away wouldn't be good. I don't want to break the law," Mary said, "just bypass it a little."

"I like the way you think," Stanley said. "How can we help?"

"Rosie, I need to borrow your portable mannequin," Mary said, opening the emergency box Rosie placed on the table.

She drew out the inflatable doll. "I need a stand-in for the afternoon."

"What the hell is that?" Stanley asked, turning on Rosie.

"What does it look like?" Rosie replied.

"It looks like trouble," Stanley said, blushing from his collar up. "Pure and simple trouble."

Mary laughed and walked over to the storefront windows. She closed the blinds securely and then brushed her hands together briskly. "So, Stanley, do you want to help dress her or would you like another task?"

Stanley's blush deepened. "You want me to do something, tell me quick, because I am leaving," he said, moving toward the door.

"Wait, wait, I'm sorry," Mary said. "What I really need is to borrow your car. I have to keep my car out front to make it look like I'm still here."

"Can you drive a stick-shift?" Stanley asked, his grizzled white eyebrow rising halfway up his forehead.

"Is the Pope Catholic?" Mary responded. "Of course I can drive a stick. My daddy taught me how to drive a real car."

Stanley nodded and smiled. "Okay, then," he said. "I'll pull Betsey up behind the back of the store. The keys will be in the visor. But I ain't coming back in here 'til that thing is packed back up in the box."

Rosie laughed. "Then get yourself out of here because I don't have all day to wait before we inflate her."

Stanley rushed to the door. "I'm gone," he said. "Mary, the car will be waiting for you in ten minutes."

"Thanks, Stanley, I appreciate it," she said.

Rosie pulled out a battery powered pump and inflated the life-sized doll. The doll's arms and legs stuck out stiffly in sixty degree angles and her neck seemed to be about the same diameter as her head. The dimensions of her breasts, waist and hips reminded Mary of a life-sized Barbie doll.

"Wow, if she were real – she'd have major back issues," Mary said. "No one better see her from the front – they'd never believe that was me."

"What is she going to be wearing?" Rosie asked.

Mary opened her closet door and pulled out a t-shirt and jeans, then she slipped out of the jacket she'd been wearing. "I thought dressy casual," Mary laughed. "Do you think they'll fit?"

Rosie looked at Mary and then looked back at the doll. "Well, hopefully they'll stretch."

They pulled the t-shirt over the doll's head and stuffed the arms through the sleeves. Rosie laid the doll on the desk and Mary pulled the jeans up the legs and buttoned them at the waist. It took both of them to maneuver the arms into the jacket.

"Wow, that was harder than I thought," Mary said. "So what do we do for her head?"

Rosie pulled a wig out of her box that was similar in shade to Mary's hair. "This ought to do the trick, but it's not the same cut," Rosie said with a sigh. "Was that police officer a male or female?"

"A male," Mary answered.

"Oh, then he'll never notice anyway," she laughed.

With the wig Velcroed in place, they stood back and looked at their creation. "Damn, we've built one of Charlie's Angels," Rosie said.

Mary laughed. "Now all we have to do it get her to sit at my desk for the day and we're set."

Rosie picked up the doll and positioned it over the chair. Mary grabbed it by the waist and stuffed it into the chair and quickly moved the chair against the desk. But no sooner had she stepped away, the doll straightened in the chair and pushed away from the desk.

"Okay, that's not going to work," Mary said.

"I have the perfect solution," Rosie said.

She pulled a scarf from her box and wrapped it around the doll's waist, and then she tied it tightly to the bottom of the chair. "Viola, seat belts," she said.

Mary pushed the chair up to the desk and positioned the doll's hands so they looked like they were typing on the keyboard. "Can't get much better than this," Mary said. "Rosie, you are a genius."

"Thanks, sweetie," Rosie said. "I am always here for you. But let me ask you one thing, does Chief Alden have a good reason for worrying about you?"

Mary gave Rosie a quick hug. "I'll be fine," she said.

"Don't you think I didn't catch that you didn't give me an answer to my question," Rosie said, placing her hand on Mary's arm. "At least tell me where you plan to go and how long you plan on being there, just in case."

"Don't worry, Rosie," Mary replied. "I'm just going for a walk in the woods. What could happen?"

Rosie didn't look convinced.

"I have my cell phone," Mary said. "If there's any trouble I'll call you or Stanley, okay?"

Rosie nodded. "You scoot out the back and I'll wait a few minutes, open the blinds and then walk over to my store," she said. "I'll come over and close up for you too."

"You're the best," Mary said.

She scooped up her purse and a small backpack and closed the back door softly behind her.

True to his word, Stanley had left "Betsey" behind the building. Betsey was a turquoise blue 1961 Chevy Impala four-door sedan. She was the size of a boat and had the engine power of a locomotive. Stanley bought her new when he and his wife were newlyweds, and with Stanley's care and devotion she ran as smoothly today as she had fifty years ago.

Mary slipped into the front seat and smiled when she saw the felt hat and jacket Stanley had left for her on the white leather bench seat. She popped the hat on her head and then pulled the visor down. A pair of keys with a red diamond-shaped plastic key chain that advertised Wagner's Office Products with a phone number of Pencil 2-3489 fell into her hands. She slipped the key into the ignition and turned it, the engine purred to life.

She stepped down on the clutch, shifted into reverse and carefully maneuvered the car into the alley. Then she shifted into first and crept down to the end of the block. She scanned the street. No police officers in view. Good! She slunk down in the seat, let up on the clutch and drove slowly away from downtown Freeport.

Once she was at the intersection of Highway 26 and Galena Street, she felt a little safer. She slid into the right lane and flicked on her turn signal. There were three cars in front of her. The drive down Highway 26 to Highway 20 was only about a mile and once she was on Highway 20, she was free. The light seemed to be taking forever. Mary tapped on the steering wheel, waiting for the green. She glanced into the rearview mirror and her heart jumped when she saw Bradley's cruiser pulling onto Galena Street several blocks behind her.

"Come on, come on, come on," she whispered desperately.

She glanced around, frantically considering her options. Everyone in town knew that this was Stanley's car and they would assume that he was driving it. Assume until they pulled up alongside and saw Mary. Mary glanced back again. He was getting closer. *Think, think, think.* She could pull into the Pizza Place parking lot, but Bradley could follow her in there. She could try to change lanes and make a left turn, but it was fairly impossible with the huge car. She could bend over and pretend she was picking something up, but Bradley might think that Stanley was in trouble and stop to offer assistance.

Glancing back she saw that he was about a half a block behind her. *Crap!* But when she looked forward, the light had turned and all three cars had already cleared the intersection. Mary accelerated and turned onto Highway 26. She was more than a quarter mile down the road when the cruiser crossed the intersection and continued down Galena. Mary breathed a sigh of relief and headed toward Apple River Fort with a smile on her face.

She pulled into a parking space at the far corner of the lot. Not only because it helped to protect Stanley's precious Betsey, but it also brought her closer to the area where the shed used to be. She slipped on the jacket Stanley had left her and grabbed the backpack. Opening it, she quickly scanned the contents: water bottle, compass, flashlight, Swiss Army knife and bug repellant. Tossing the keys and her cell phone into the pack, she closed it up and as she exited the car, hitched it onto her shoulder. She locked up Betsey and walked toward the edge of the woods.

The grass was covered with autumn leaves and there was definitely a chill in the air. She shoved her hands into her pockets and glanced up at the sky. Dark clouds were lining the horizon and Mary guessed she had about two hours before the storm arrived.

Stopping at the edge of the woods she looked back up the hill toward the main street. She tried to remember how things looked when she had chased Jessica on her bicycle.

"I think the path was somewhere around here," she said, pushing through some brush and stepping onto a narrow deer path. The woods closed in around her. The sounds from the traffic at the top of the hill faded away and Mary felt very alone. "Okay, I see ghosts for a living," she whispered. "It's kind of silly to be afraid of the woods."

A cloud drifted over the afternoon sun and the woods darkened. "Maybe not so silly," she amended, reaching into her backpack and pulling out the flashlight.

Chapter Twenty-three

Something wasn't right. Bradley pulled his cruiser into his parking space at City Hall and threw it into park. He hated when he got these nagging feelings, but something definitely wasn't right.

Could I just be feeling guilty? he wondered as he climbed up the stairs to his second-floor office. *Mary is a trained professional, after all, and she has a job to do. But damn it, she's been shot at, accused of being a terrorist and she ran into a fort... I still don't quite understand the fort thing...but she obviously encountered quite a few dangerous situations. She needs my help.*

"Whether she likes it or not," he muttered.

"I'm sorry, Chief, did you say something?" his administrative assistant, Dorothy, asked.

I am going nuts, he thought.

He shook his head and smiled. "No, Dorothy, just thinking out loud."

She smiled back, but he thought it had an "I need to be nice to the crazy guy" edge to it.

He stopped at his office doorway and looked back at Dorothy, now busily typing up some reports, and shook his head.

If she thinks I'm crazy, he decided silently, *maybe she'll work harder to keep me happy.*

He logged on to his computer, glanced over his e-mails and finally, did what he'd been anxious to do since this morning, place a call to the officer who was watching Mary.

"Everton, this is Chief Alden," he said after the officer had picked up the call. "How are things going with O'Reilly?"

Everton didn't even try to hide the boredom in his voice. *Obviously he doesn't think I'm crazy,* Bradley thought.

"The subject has not left her office since 13:30," Everton reported. "She hasn't even left her desk."

Bradley glanced up at the clock. It was nearly four-thirty. She hadn't left her desk for three hours?

"Everton, did she have any visitors?"

"Yes, sir," he responded dully. "She received two visitors soon after she arrived at her office, Stanley Wagner and Rosie Pettigrew. They both left by 14:00 hours."

Bradley remembered seeing Stanley's car heading out of town earlier that afternoon.

"Have you seen Stanley since?" he asked.

He could hear the yawn in the young officer's voice. "Yes, sir, Stanley has been sitting in front of his store all afternoon, as usual."

"Everton, get your ass out of the car and enter Miss O'Reilly's place of business," he yelled, hoping that got a response out of the young man. "I want an immediate report. Got it?"

"Yes. Yes, sir," came the frightened reply.

"Good. Now he can think I'm crazy too," Bradley muttered, tapping his fingers on his desk as he waited for the report.

"Sir, Chief Alden," the panicked voice on the other end of the line caused Bradley's stomach to clench. "She's not there, sir. It was a doll, an inflatable doll."

"Damn," Bradley growled. "You get back on that street and don't let Stanley or Rosie sneak away. I've got some questions for them."

One thing I know for sure, he thought as he grabbed his keys, revolver and phone. *If I'm not already crazy, Mary O'Reilly is going to drive me there.*

Chapter Twenty-four

Mary moved cautiously into the depths of the woods, stopping every few feet to survey the area and try to catch a glimpse of either Jessica or one of the other little girls. A scurrying sound in the brush had her dropping to the ground behind a large log. "Okay, Mary, calm down," she said, taking a deep breath. "This is just a lovely forested area. Bambi could live here."

"Then again, Bambi's mother did die," she countered.

Suddenly, the woods came alive with sunshine and activity. Birds were chirping and a warm wind was blowing through the trees. The sun was warm on her back and Mary started to perspire. *What the hell?* she wondered, looking up to the blue sky.

Mary looked through the woods and saw Jessica about fifty yards away floating in the air. She was struggling, beating her fists and twisting her body, but the unseen abductor held her tight. Mary jumped up and ran toward Jessica, swerving around trees and brush, working desperately to keep her in sight.

The abductor moved quickly. Mary could tell that he was familiar with his surroundings. He definitely knew where he was going. Mary scanned the area and tried to gauge where he was heading with the little girl.

In the distance she could see an old cabin; it must be the one the paramedic mentioned. He had thought it was haunted. A chill ran up Mary's spine – the abductor was taking Jessica to the cabin.

Mary stopped for a moment, her breath coming out in gasps. She did another quick surveillance of the area. If she ran to the top of the small ridge in the distance, she might gain on Jessica's abductor. She turned and sprinted up the hill toward the ridge.

The path up the hill was overgrown, with brush and roots creating an uneven and hazardous surface. Mary felt like she was back in Rookie Boot Camp, hopping through the tire obstacle course, no sooner had she placed one foot down than she leapt up on the next. She watched the ground, only glancing up occasionally to be sure that she was still on course. The way was fairly clear with the only impediment, a sapling at the very edge of the path, about five yards ahead.

She continued quickly, but moments later her shoulder hit the tree and knocked her to the ground.

"Damn, that's twice," she muttered, wiping the cold rain from her eyes and seeing the tree in its full-grown, twenty-four years later version.

Her vision wavered between present day and twenty-four years ago, the sapling aging before her eyes. Then it stopped and she was left at present day.

In cold rain and a darkening sky rather than the Indian Summer Day that Jessica was snatched.

She stood and looked around. The former ridge had been excavated and now had a steep drop-off.

"Crap," she shouted and raced through the rain to the top of the hill.

She looked around and could picture where the old cabin would have stood. She was only about a mile away from her location.

She ran along the edge of the ridge her feet slipping on the wet leaves, trying to find an area that was not as steep, so she could reach the bottom of the small valley. About one-hundred yards closer to her destination, she found a place that had been graded for run-off. Loose river rocks covered the ground and would make Mary's descent hazardous, but it was the only way she was going reach the cabin quickly.

She stepped onto the rocks, the ground slipping underneath her feet, and let the momentum of the rock slide work with her angled movements. Slipping and sliding, rain beating against her jacket and head, she balanced her body like a surfer and half-ran, half-slipped down the incline. With only three feet to go, she leapt forward and landed on solid ground.

She turned toward the direction of the old cabin and ran through the woods. The rain increased as lightning flashed across the sky and thunder rumbled all around her. Trees tossed in the wind as the remaining autumn leaves were torn from the branches and sailed through the air.

Mary pushed against the wind, putting all of her strength into moving forward. Her jacket was soaked and plastered against her body. Water streamed in rivulets from her hair down her face and neck. Finally, she entered a clearing that seemed like it was the right spot for the cabin. "Come on, Jessica," she said, her hands on her knees as she gasped for air. "Help me see you. I want to help."

Suddenly the rain disappeared and the sun was out again. Mary could see the cabin a few feet away. She took a deep breath, straightened and jogged to the cabin's door.

She reached out to grab the doorknob when it was snatched away as the door crashed open. Jessica's motionless form drifted through the doorway, her arms and legs hanging at her side. Mary covered her mouth with her hand and bit back a sob.

"No, damn it! No," she cried.

She leapt toward the still moving body when suddenly, it disappeared. She stopped and looked around. "Jessica! Jessica! Where are you?" she called.

The sun was still shining. The sky was still bright. But Jessica had disappeared from view.

"What the hell...?" she began, but a sharp stinging sensation on her arm interrupted her thought process and brought her immediately back to present day.

Luckily the second bullet missed her and exploded into the tree next to her. She immediately dropped to the muddy ground. Rain poured over her in the dim early evening light and her arm throbbed. "Well, damn, what next?"

"Over here."

"What?"

Mary turned toward the youthful voice. There in the mist of the forest were four little girls, all about eight years old, all with long, dark hair, all similar enough that they could have been sisters. And all ghosts.

"The bad man is coming," one of the girls called. "Follow us so he won't get you."

Mary could hear the sounds of movement from the woods, but the light was too dim to see what was coming. She instinctively reached for her weapon, then remembered she was a civilian and her gun was safely locked in the gun safe next to her bed.

"Quick, he's coming!" the little ghost urged, her pale skin iridescent in the twilight.

"What the hell," Mary muttered and belly crawled to the cover of the woods where the girls waited.

"He's a very bad man," another of the girls said once Mary reached the shelter of the woods.

"He hurt me," another added, her large brown eyes glistening with tears. "I can't find my mom."

Mary wanted to gather them into her arms, but she knew that she would only find mist, not the corporeal children they represented. "I'll help you. I promise," she whispered.

"We need to go now," the first girl said urgently. "He's coming."

They turned and led her through a small, hidden break in the dense brush and through a tunnel of overgrown bushes and tangled branches. Mary bent over and moved as quickly as possible, following the girls as they drifted over the uneven ground.

The foliage was dense and the storm had covered the late afternoon sun, so Mary was left relying on the glow emitted from the girls' unearthly forms and her flashlight.

She could still hear the patter of the rain against the leaves, but very little rain reached her. The ground beneath her feet was covered with a collection of dried leaves, pine needles and soft dirt. One of the little girls turned back to Mary. "He can't get us in here," she said with a shy smile. "He's too scared."

The other girls giggled in response and then continued leading Mary further into the woods.

Chapter Twenty-five

"The bad man is still coming," one of the girls said, the others listened for a moment and nodded.

Mary stopped, she could hear the rain hitting against the vegetation and the rumbling of thunder in the distance, but she couldn't hear anything else. She closed her eyes and concentrated. There it was, the almost imperceptible sound of shoes meeting muddy ground. It had a rhythm all its own and they were right, it was getting closer.

She ripped a piece of lining from Stanley's jacket and wrapped it around her arm to staunch the blood flow. *It's only a flesh wound*, she thought and nearly laughed out loud at the cliché.

Pulling her cell phone out of the backpack she flipped it open and looked. No bars. Well, she wasn't exactly surprised. So she wasn't going to be able to call the cavalry.

Mary felt a cold chill on her arm. She looked down. The girl who had mentioned her mother had placed a hand on Mary's arm. "We have to hurry," she whispered urgently.

Mary nodded and followed the girls once again. She peered ahead and could see that the carefully crafted tunnel would soon open into a clearing. At that point, she would be an easy target for her pursuer. The girls understood the dilemma.

"We'll go first and run," one said. "He'll chase us and then we can disappear. You run the other way."

Mary instinctively shook her head. "No," she said firmly, "I won't sacrifice any of you to get away."

The smallest one giggled softly. "You're nice. But he can't hurt us anymore," she said. "And we need you to help us."

Mary took a deep breath and nodded. They were right, but it still seemed wrong. "Okay," she finally said, "let's wait until he gets closer and then you run to the left. As soon as I hear him chasing you, I'll run to the right."

The girls nodded solemnly. "There's a big tunnel that goes back up the hill," one of the girls said. "If you find that, you can climb in it and be safe."

They all walked to the edge of the clearing. The lightning flashed all around them and the rain was coming down in sheets. The girls' little faces, more luminous as the sky had darkened, turned to her. "Don't forget," they whispered, and then darted out into the rain and out of sight.

Mary waited. She heard a shot ricochet off a tree in the direction the girls had run. This was her chance. She bent low and darted out of the tunnel toward the thicket of trees about forty yards away. The rain pelted her face as she ran with all of her strength toward the cover of the woods. The ground was slick with rain and mud and tree branches whipped back and forth in the wind. Lightning exploded behind her. She prayed that she wasn't the tallest thing in the clearing – but she wasn't going to take the time to look.

She heard another shot in the opposite direction, breathed a quick sigh of relief, and ran harder. She was almost to the woods when another shot exploded, this time only a few yards away from her. She dove into the brush and rolled behind a log for cover. Another bullet slammed into the tree trunk behind her. "Well, damn," she muttered. "Now what?"

She peered over the log. She could see a figure in the distance, but the rain was too fierce for her to get a good look at him. "Where's a good lightning bolt when you need one?" she murmured as she watched him slowly move forward.

Off to her left Mary noticed a dim light moving through the woods. Was it the girls again? At this point, there was really nothing they could do. She glanced back to the gunman. He was staying at the edge of the woods, making his way slowly around the circumference of the field toward her. The light to the left was getting brighter. Did the gunman have an accomplice? At this point, she was almost dead center between the two. "Dead center – bad choice of words, Mary," she chided herself.

She watched and waited. Both figures moving closer. Neither one seemed to be aware of the other.

As the light came closer to the edge of the woods, Mary noticed that the gunman had stopped in his tracks. He moved away from the outer clearing and into the brush. Mary turned frantically to find him in the dark rain. He was still there – waiting, but mostly hidden in the branches of a large oak.

The person carrying the light moved into the clearing. Even through the pounding rain, his half-run looked familiar. He stopped and gazed around the clearing.

"Mary O'Reilly," Bradley shouted. "This is Police Chief Bradley Alden of the Freeport Police Department. Please acknowledge your whereabouts."

Mary's quick relief turned to panic as she realized that he was an open target for the gunman. "Bradley," she shouted. "Get down! Gunman!"

Bradley dropped to the ground. She could see him pull out his revolver and scan the area. The blast of tree bark above her head was a clear reminder that she had given away her position when she called out.

She dropped to the ground and looked around. Several yards away was a huge fallen log that could provide protection. She decided that she would figure out how to get to the other side of it once she got there.

She crawled along the muddy ground, raindrops ricocheting onto her face. Her clothes were soaked all the way through and she was chilled to the bone. She finally reached the log, an ancient oak with a number of large branches on either side.

She examined the positioning of the log and could see a small hollow underneath. Several of the large branches held the log up enough to form a fairly substantial passageway. Mary was sure she could squeeze under and get safely through to the other side, away from the gunman.

She reached her arms through the opening and grabbed hold of some branches on the other side of the tree and began to pull herself through. Mud, stones and bark scraped her sides. Her arm throbbed, but she continued to pull.

Halfway through, she realized that the opening might not be large enough to fit her hips. She tugged. She was stuck tight.

"Damn, damn, damn, damn," she whimpered, as rain poured down upon her.

"Need some help?"

She looked up through the rain to see a fairly smug Bradley Alden standing over her. Relief warred with pain.

"No, really, I'm fine," she snapped. "What the hell do you think?"

He squatted down in front of her, rain pouring off the brim of his cap. "Well, I thought perhaps you had the same amazing trait as the Mary O'Reilly we found in your office," he replied, "the ability to deflate."

Chapter Twenty-six

Freezing, Mary shivered beneath a police-issued wool blanket in the front seat of the cruiser while Bradley reported the information to the Jo Davies County Sheriff's Department.

"From the look of the slug, it's the same caliber of weapon that was used earlier this week in a similar shooting," he said.

He listened for a moment and then looked directly at Mary as he spoke into the phone. "Yes, the intended victim is going to be placed under twenty-four-hour surveillance. Yes, she has agreed to the surveillance."

He raised his eyebrow, daring her to disagree. Mary sighed and nodded. *Okay,* she thought, *someone tried to kill me twice, maybe I should give in a little.*

"Yes, her wound has been cared for," he said.

Mary winced, remembering the sting of the antiseptic ointment Bradley had applied just before bandaging the two-inch scrape.

"Thanks, yeah, I appreciate it," he continued. "No, no idea. Male. Probably over six feet – but even though the victim is trained, the rain was coming down too hard for her to get a good visual. Yeah, he was out of here after his last attempt. I looked for tracks, but couldn't find any. Yeah, maybe your guys will have better luck.

"I'll send some of my guys back tomorrow for her car," he added. "Thanks for all your help, Steve."

Bradley finished the conversation, clicked off the phone and turned to Mary. "They're probably not going to find tracks, are they?" Mary asked, knowing the answer before he spoke.

Bradley shook his head. "I don't think so. But the weather worked in our favor. It's hard to disguise everything in this much mud. This guy is good."

Mary shivered. "And smart. He killed five little girls more than twenty-four years ago and was never caught."

Bradley shook his head. "He hasn't been caught yet," he said. "We just need to catch him…"

He stopped.

"Before he kills me," Mary finished for him.

Bradley looked at her for a moment, turned and started his car. "Not an option," he said, putting his car in gear and pulling out of the parking lot toward Freeport.

The thirty-minute ride back to Freeport was completed mostly in silence, each lost in their own thoughts. It was just past ten as they drove down Stephenson Street.

"Do you have an alarm system at your house?" Bradley finally asked.

Mary shook her head. "No, the ghosts occasionally set them off."

"Do you have a friend with a big mean dog?"

"No, ghosts tend to creep out even big mean dogs."

"Do you want to take a few days off and visit your folks in Chicago?"

Mary turned to him. "You wouldn't be suggesting I hide away and let someone else solve my case, would you?"

Bradley understood the look in her eye, but decided it was worth the risk. "Just until I can get something substantial on the creep who's after you."

Mary shook her head. "No, I can't do that, sorry."

"Mary, you've been shot at twice," he said. "Don't you think it's time...?"

"If you say it's time I leave this to the professionals, I'll shoot you."

"I was going to say, time you stepped back and protected yourself," he continued. "These girls are dead. You can't help them anymore. They've waited this long, they can wait a little longer."

He pulled up in front of her house.

"You don't understand," Mary said, picturing the faces of the little girls. "They are trapped here. They are in constant fear. They can't move on to where they are supposed to be. And they're being terrorized by this monster too. Even in death. They've waited long enough."

Mary got out of the cruiser and turned back. "Thanks for worrying, really, but I've got to see this through."

She closed the door and hurried to her front porch. As soon as she let herself in, she heard Bradley drive away.

Locking the door, she turned and leaned against it, studying the room. This house had always felt safe to her, even when she had nocturnal visitors like Earl, she'd never been afraid of being alone. But she had to admit that tonight she was a little jittery. She took a deep breath. There was no way someone was going to intimidate her in her own home.

"Screw this," she said aloud and moved into the front room.

The glow from the streetlight outside her house filled the room with enough light that Mary could see the shadows of her furniture. She softly walked forward, stopping at the base of the staircase.

Standing still, she listened to see if there were any discordant sounds. She waited for a few moments and then carefully climbed the staircase, keeping to the edges to avoid making noise. At the top she slid along the wall and made her way to her bedroom.

The door was ajar. *I probably left it open*, she thought. Mary glanced around the room; the shadows were familiar and nothing seemed out of place. She moved to the nightstand and knelt in front of it. Pulling open the drawer, she entered the combination of the safe and, when the small door opened, she reached in and pulled out her Colt 1911 semi-automatic pistol. She weighed it her hand. The cool, smooth metal felt familiar and comforting.

Looking down, she noticed the answering machine on top of the nightstand was blinking. She clicked back the caller ID; the number was blocked. Her heart pounded. She pressed the button to play the message.

"Line one, one new message, Saturday nine-forty-two p.m.," the machine responded.

"You are mine. You were meant to be mine. Just like the others. I am coming for you."

Mary's hand shook for a moment. The voice had been electronically manipulated and Mary knew, from past experience, that the message had been too short to have left any clues.

Fury replaced fear. Mary reached back into the safe, pulled out the handgun's magazine and slapped it into the gun.

"Bring it."

She brought the gun into the bathroom with her, placed it inside the cabinet near the shower and turned to make the adjustments on the shower's control panel.

Her full body shower consisted of five sets of vertically mounted spray nozzles that sprayed her body from head to toe. She was able to adjust the volume, the type of spray, the pressure and the temperature. It was like being in heaven.

Hot water and a massage spray, she decided, would help ease the ache and cold from her body. She could hardly wait.

She took off her clothes and placed them in a wicker hamper. Then she stepped into the shower and closed her eyes, bracing her hands on the shower wall in front of her as she let the pulsating heat of the shower ease the chill and tension out of her body. Droplets of water beaded on her bandaged arm. Steam rose all around her, coating the shower stall with an opaque blanket. She felt some of the terror of the night begin to slip away.

Chapter Twenty-seven

She was not his problem. She was an adult. She could make her own decisions. She was a professional. She could handle herself. She understood the criminal mind. She wasn't going to make another mistake.

"Damn it," Bradley stomped on the brake and pulled the cruiser to the side of the road. What the hell was he going to do about this situation?

He pulled out his phone and called the Jo Davies Sheriff, maybe he could shed some light on the case.

"Hey, Steve, this is Alden," he said. "Did you get anywhere with the shooter this evening? Any leads?"

"My deputies and I have been out there for the past hour," the sheriff said. "No one saw anything. But considering the weather…"

"Yeah, you're right, there are not a lot of witnesses during a thunderstorm," he agreed.

"Don't know if this is helpful," the sheriff added, "but my guys did a walk-through in the area of the shooting, and this guy was definitely stalking your vic. This was not a random poacher just shooting in the wrong direction; this guy followed her for a long time."

"What did they find?" Bradley asked.

"Some vegetation was crushed down enough to tell that he was watching and waiting for quite a while," the sheriff replied. "Then there was a place where he lost her, and then doubled back to where he finally just about caught her. This guy was good, he knew what he was doing. I'd make sure I keep an eye on that lady, 'cause this guy is on her trail."

"Thanks, Steve, that's exactly what I needed to hear," Bradley said, making a U-turn and heading back to Mary's house. "Keep me informed, okay?"

Bradley pulled into the driveway and jogged over to the porch. It was strange that she hadn't turned on any lights yet. He knocked on the door and waited. He felt the hairs on the back of his neck raise, something was wrong.

This time he pounded on the door. "Mary, it's Bradley. Open the door."

Chapter Twenty-eight

The pounding on the front door startled Mary. She turned and shampoo dripped into her eyes. Swearing, she tried unsuccessfully to clear her vision. Blindly, she reached forward and turned off the water.

She opened the shower door just a crack and reached one arm out for her towel. She found the thick terry cloth, rubbed her eyes and was finally was able to see. Through the steam she thought she saw a quick movement in the mirror. Her heart jumped. *What the hell?*

It was too early for Earl to come. Besides, Earl should be safely home by now. Did another ghostly visitor take his place?

She paused, wrapped the towel around her body and tucked the end in securely. She slid the shower door the rest of the way open, and steam escaped into the room, clouding the mirror even more. Never allowing her eyes to move from the mirror, she reached over and slid the cabinet door open, grasping around the inside for her gun. Finally, she felt it and drew it to her chest.

She waited, listening for any sounds, peering through the steam for any movement. A second round of pounding on the front door jolted her. She took a deep breath, shook her head and felt fairly foolish.

The movement in the mirror must have been her imagination.

She stepped forward, then stopped. The muddied footprint was large. The tracks were from a man's boot. And it was right outside her shower door.

She leaned back against the bathroom wall, her hand over her mouth. He had been right there. Watching her shower. She felt sick to her stomach.

She couldn't move. The pounding continued, but all she could do was stare at the print on the floor.

The phone rang in her bedroom. She lifted her head and stared across the room. He had been on the phone. He had warned her that he was coming for her. She heard her voice answer, "Hi, this is Mary, sorry I'm not here. Leave a message."

"Mary, it's Bradley. I'm downstairs pounding on your door. Get down here and open the door or I'm letting myself in."

"Bradley," she whispered.

Blood pounding in her temples, she skirted the tracks on the floor and quickly made her way back down the stairs. She could see his tracks on the sides of her steps – mimicking her earlier attempt to walk up the stairs noiselessly. She reached the kitchen and felt a cold draft from the open kitchen door.

"Mary! Mary! Answer the damn door," Bradley shouted from the other side of the front door.

She moved away from the kitchen, backing away from the open door and ran quickly to the front. She unlatched the deadbolt and threw open the door.

"Hey, sorry," Bradley said, when he saw what she was wearing. "I didn't realize..."

Then he saw her face and her grip on the gun.

"What happened?" he said, closing the door behind him and instinctively moving in front of Mary.

She took a deep breath. "He was here," she said, her breath coming out in hitches. "He was in my bathroom. He was watching me while I was in the shower."

"Shit," Bradley swore. "Stay here, I'll check the house."

Mary shook her head. "He's gone. Back door. He must have heard you."

He pulled out his phone and punched in some numbers. "I have a 10-25 – Breaking and Entering," he began, repeating Mary's address. "I want a forensic unit here immediately, along with some officers to scour the area for any suspicious persons. Alden. Out."

He put his phone away and turned to Mary. She was standing in the middle of the living room, clasping the towel to her breast and looking lost.

"How are you doing?" he asked softly.

She shivered and shook her head. "I'm feeling a little overwhelmed," she replied.

"Yeah, I can imagine," he moved over to her. "Cold?"

She nodded. "Yeah, a little."

"I don't want you to go upstairs just yet," Bradley said. "We need to check for prints. Do you have anything down here that you can put on to keep warm?"

Mary motioned to the hall closet. "I have an overcoat in there," she said.

Bradley moved to the door. "Mary, do me a favor and stand over in that corner," he motioned with his head, moving her away from the line of sight of the closet, just in case her intruder really hadn't left the house.

He pulled the door open, his gun ready, and found no one in the closet.

"Which coat?" he asked, amazed at the number of different options hanging before him.

"This one," she said, coming up beside him, tugging a London Fog trench coat off a hanger, slipping the coat over her towel and tying it securely.

"So, the bad guy isn't in my closet," she said, taking a deep breath and trying to calm her nerves.

He nodded. Yeah," he replied, glancing around the room.

She knew what he wanted. He wanted to check the rest of the house. He knew, as well as she did, that the intruder could have only made it look like he had left. Waiting for another opportunity to get to his victim. And she was the potential victim.

She sat on the arm of the recliner to hide the weakness in her knees. She knew Bradley wanted to search, but she wasn't quite ready to be alone yet.

"Do you want me to sit someplace safe so you can check out the rest of the house?" she asked.

He looked at her; she could see the doubt in his eyes. "And you would you be willing to do that?"

She actually smiled, feeling slightly better. "No, but I would be happy to back you up while you do it."

He nodded. "Just until my guys come," he said. "Then you have to pretend that I'm in charge."

Chapter Twenty-nine

Michael Strong had a secret. A secret he had worked hard to keep. He did everything that was expected of him. As a young man, he had done an exemplary job on the senator's campaign. That experience, and his family's connections, had moved him up quickly in the financial and political community. He had married well and had taken his rightful position in society.

Mike was President of the Freeport State Bank. He was on the board of a number of charitable organizations in town, as well as an advisor on a few municipal task forces. He was bright, charming, well-liked, and, he reminded himself, easily recognizable.

He drove through the poorer section of town, keeping to the side streets until he merged onto the Beltline that led over to Highway 20. He accelerated and entered the Highway, heading west for only a mile or so. Then he exited on Highway 75 and continued north.

The darkness of the rural road comforted him. No one would be able to recognize him or his car. The softly falling rain encouraged him. No one would be out on a night like this. No one would learn his secret.

He thought about his wife, tucked into bed, waiting for him to get home from a late meeting. She didn't suspect anything. How many years had he being lying to her?

He stopped himself. He wasn't lying. He was keeping this from her to protect her, protect his family, and protect his position in the community. Really, this was all for them, he reasoned.

The neon lights from Flagstaff's Bar and Grill glowed with welcome warmth. He felt the tension leave his body. This was his place; he knew he was always welcome here. They understood him here.

He pulled up onto the rough gravel parking lot. The neon sign reflected in the puddles and the rain poured down the side of the building where the gutters had long since disappeared. He walked to the door, caught his reflection in the glass.

He had been the wonder boy. Tall, athletic, blonde and intelligent. He was every high school girl's dream and he had taken advantage of their adulation, as had been expected.

His parents had expected so much – demanded so much. He had a name to carry on, a reputation to honor, and a legacy that bore responsibility.

But no one asked him what he wanted. No one asked him how he felt. If they had known, he would have been ostracized and abandoned. His schooling, his position and his future would have been jeopardized. He couldn't have that – so he lived a lie.

The lights were dim inside the bar. There were booths discreetly placed so private conversations were indeed private. He walked to the bar and placed his order. "The usual, Mac," he said with a smile.

Mac understood that the success of his business depended on his ability to be discreet. Mike understood more than most that money was a great motivator.

"Sure thing, Mike," Mac replied. "There's someone waiting for you at booth nine – you want me to bring it there?"

Mike nodded, a little intrigued. "Yes, certainly. That would be great."

He walked across the room, slipped into booth nine and gasped in surprise at the man sitting across from him.

"I never knew," Mike said.

The gentleman cut him off. "You still don't," he replied. "And if you want me to keep your dirty little secret, you'll never mention this meeting to anyone."

He was soaked to the skin and muddy. There was dirt on his face, and if he hadn't known him for more than twenty-four years he would have never recognized him.

"Hank, how did you find out about me?" he asked.

"I knew you were gay from the moment I met you, way back when we worked on the senator's campaign together," Hank replied. "It's not that hard to see."

"But if you know, who else...?"

Hank cut him off again. "Most people don't see the way I do," he said. "Your secret is safe, as long as I want it to be."

Mike leaned across the table. "Don't joke about this Hank," he said. "If people found out...if my parents found out..."

"You'd send them to an early grave," Hank chuckled. "And then you'd finally get all of their money. You should have outed yourself a long time ago."

"Hank, this isn't a laughing matter," Mike replied.

Hank stopped laughing. He sat back in the booth, hidden by the shadows as the bartender brought Mike his beer. "You need anything else?" the bartender asked.

"No. No, Mac, we're good. Thanks," Mike replied.

"What do you want from me?" Mike asked, once the bartender had walked away.

Hank reached over and pulled Mike's beer across the table, took a sip, fiddled with the tall glass for a moment and then pushed it back to Mike.

"I need you to do me a favor," Hank replied, "that's all."

"Just a favor? Why did you have to come out here and ask me? You could have just as easily stopped by the office."

Hank shrugged. "We both have our reasons to keep certain areas of our lives private," he said pointedly. "Don't we, Mikey?"

Mike felt his skin heat with the flush of anger. He had always hated that nickname and, as he recalled, Hank had always enjoyed using it.

"What do you want?"

"I need some help, some financial advice, that's all," he said.

"I do this and you never mention seeing me here?" he questioned. "Right? You never even hint about it?"

Hank smiled and Mike shivered, reminded of the alligator at the zoo – cold, calculating and patient.

"If you do this, you will have enough on me that you won't ever have to worry about me," he said. "Of course, that's the risk I take. But I trust you Mike. I trust you with my life."

Maybe he had misjudged Hank. Maybe he was nervous. Maybe he just needed a friend.

Mike nodded. "Yeah, I can help you," he said.

Hank stood, keeping his face in the shadows. "Okay, I'll leave now. You finish your drink, I don't want to interrupt your down time. Why don't you drive over to my office once you're done here?"

"It's awfully stormy out there," Mike added, hesitating. "Can't we do this on another night?"

Hank shook his head. "No, it really has to be tonight."

Mike sighed and took a sip of his beer. "Okay, I'll be there. Let me just finish this."

Hank smiled. "I knew I could count on you."

Chapter Thirty

The sun was barely peeking through the curtains when Mary woke up the next morning. She stretched her arms over her head and groaned. She was stiff and sore. Her entire body ached.

She shifted her position and got caught up in her clothes. *What am I wearing?* she wondered, and looked down to see her trench coat wrapped around her, definitely looking like someone slept in it.

Memories of the night before rushed through her mind. The police had been understanding and professional. Her entire house had been dusted for prints, photographed and searched in record time. The initial report had determined that her intruder had known what he was up to and left no evidence except for the muddy footprints. She almost felt that he had left those on purpose. Psychological warfare.

She remembered that after they had done all they could, Bradley had volunteered to make her a cup of tea while she sat on the couch. That was the last thing she remembered.

She got up and walked to the bathroom. The muddy footprint, still visible on her white tiled floor, stopped her at the door. She stared at the print with a mixture of fear and resentment.

Who was this monster that violated her most private space?

What were his thoughts when he was standing there watching her?

What would he have done if Bradley hadn't knocked on the door just when he had?

Her hand crept to her throat and her face paled as she imagined the possibilities.

"Good morning."

Mary jumped and spun around. Bradley stood leaning on the bedroom doorframe. "I wondered when you would finally wake up," he added.

"Wake up?" she stammered, confused.

"It's after nine," he replied. "I thought you were going to sleep all day."

"You've been here all night?"

He rolled his eyes and sighed. "Do you honestly believe that I would leave you alone after last night?"

She smiled sheepishly. "Thanks... For everything."

He shrugged. "No problem," he said. "Now, you need to move out of the way."

"What...?"

She was actually speechless when she saw Bradley retrieve a mop and bucket from the hallway and carry it past her.

"What are you doing?" she finally asked.

"I'm mopping your bathroom," he replied simply, putting his words into action.

"But why?"

"Because you don't need this reminder to haunt you any longer," he paused and smiled up at her, "if you'll forgive the pun."

She smiled back at him. "But I could…"

"Of course you could," he interrupted. "But I wanted to do this for you."

She looked around the room, not sure what she should do next.

"Why don't you go downstairs and use the guest bathroom?" he suggested. "I'll be done here in a few minutes."

She nodded. "Thanks, I will."

She grabbed her toiletries and a change of clothes. She hesitated at the top of the stairs and saw, to her relief, that the other traces from the night before had already been removed. Courtesy of Bradley Alden, she was sure.

Bright sunshine streaming through her kitchen windows dispelled the rest of the shadows. Mary actually smiled as she walked through the kitchen to the guest bath.

A half-hour later she felt like a new woman. She walked out of the bathroom to the smells of breakfast.

"What are you doing?" she asked.

Bradley stood at the stove with a pan of bacon frying on one burner and some eggs scrambling on another. "Has anyone ever told you that, for a private investigator, you ask some pretty stupid questions?"

She laughed and it felt good. "Actually, I used to ask much better questions before…"

"Yeah, I know. Before you died."

"No, before I met you," she said.

"So, I have the ability to create chaos in your thought process?" he asked, lifting his eyebrows roguishly.

She laughed. "I think it might be that you are constantly surprising me."

"Keep 'em guessing. That's what I always say," he quipped, as he moved the bacon from the pan to a waiting platter. "Now sit down, breakfast is almost ready. The cup of tea I owe you from last night is on the table."

Mary slid into her chair and took a sip of the warm tea. "So, what happened to me last night?" she asked. "The last thing I remember is sitting on the couch waiting for my tea."

Bradley smiled. "Well, I was trying to impress you with my version of scintillating conversation... So naturally, you fell asleep immediately."

"How incredibly rude of me," she replied.

"Yes, I thought so too," he agreed, placing two full plates on the table. "But considering your day, I let it pass."

"That was gracious of you," she said, biting into a piece of crisp bacon.

He sat down across from her and smiled. "Yes, once again, I thought so too."

"And then you slept downstairs?" she asked.

"Yeah," he replied, rubbing his neck. "Your couch is more comfortable than your recliner, but really, you're going to have to invest in something that's a little longer if we're going to keep this up."

She reached across the table and placed her hand over his. "I don't know if I said this last night, but thank you for being at the right place at the right time several times yesterday."

He nodded and stared at her for a few moments, then slid his hand out from beneath hers. "You were lucky. We were both lucky. And we can't rely on luck anymore, Mary. You're going to have to let me in on this one."

She nodded. "Yeah, I agree."

He stopped, speechless. "Just like that? You agree?"

She nodded. "Yeah, I figure you'll up the odds in my favor."

He smiled and scooped some eggs into his mouth. "So, what's on the agenda for today?"

"I thought it might be a good idea to review the case and just lay low," Mary answered. "I'd like to enjoy a day without being someone's target practice."

"Good idea," he said. "I need to go back to my place and get my laptop, but if it's okay with you, I'll plan on working here all day."

Mary didn't want to feel the relief his statement gave her. After all, she was a one-person show, a loner, a private eye – she shouldn't look forward to working with someone.

"And I'll bring lunch," he offered. "I make a mean pot of chili."

Mary smiled and decided not to question the current circumstances, just enjoy the camaraderie. "That sounds great, I love chili. But it doesn't seem fair, since you made breakfast."

Bradley stood and picked up both plates. "So you'll owe me. Big!"

"Yeah, I will," she laughed. "If you ever need to locate a ghost, give me a call and I'll give you a discount."

The laughter quickly went out of his eyes when he turned back. "No, I don't think I'll ever need that," he replied.

"Are you okay?" she asked.

He nodded, quickly, too quickly. "I'm great," he said, sitting down once again. "Now let's talk about this case."

An hour later, Mary had given Bradley an overview of all of the different aspects of the situation. Bradley pushed back in his chair, tapping his hand on the table. "You've done a great job of getting the information pulled together," he said.

Mary smiled. "Thanks, but what I really need is to be able to go over all the pertinent data to see if anything clicks."

Bradley nodded and then glanced at his watch. "Okay, I need to change and pick up the ingredients for lunch," he said. "I'll park the cruiser at my place and walk back. That way it looks like you're alone, in case anyone wants to come by unannounced."

Mary winced.

Bradley stood up and leaned over toward Mary. "But you won't be alone," he said. "I already have an unmarked car watching your house."

"Thank you," she said, with a soft sigh of relief.

"Don't thank me until you've tasted my chili," he quipped, trying to lighten the mood.

"Oh, great, just what I need," she joked. "Another threat."

After Bradley left, Mary set her laptop up on the dining room table and pulled out a couple of new yellow legal pads. She placed all of the information she had collected over the past week in a pile on the center of the table.

An hour later, when the doorbell rang, she smiled and hurried to open the door. "You didn't have to ring..." she began, then stopped when she saw Rosie standing on the porch.

"Well, thanks, sweetie, but I always feel that ringing the doorbell is better than walking in," Rosie grinned, moving past Mary, entering her home and looking around. "You never know what you might be walking into these days."

"Rosie, please come in," Mary said.

Rosie laughed and held out a plate covered with aluminum foil. "I come bearing gifts and an inquisitive mind," she said. "Homemade cinnamon rolls for a quiet Sunday morning. And lots of questions."

Mary took the offered plate and lifted the foil. She took a deep breath of the yeasty dough and cinnamon scent and smiled. "Rosie, these are amazing."

"So what's up?" Rosie asked. "Chief Alden came looking for us at about five, he said the jig was up, the doll had deflated and he wanted to know which one of us lent you a car."

She giggled delicately. "He was quite determined," she said, waving her hand in front of her face. "So much testosterone. What happened yesterday?"

Mary sighed. "Well, it was an extraordinary day," she said, guiding Rosie into the kitchen. "Let me make us some tea, and I'll give you all of the details."

Rosie sat on a bar stool next to the counter and nodded. "It smells like you've already had your breakfast," she said. "That's pretty ambitious for a lazy Sunday morning."

Mary shrugged as she filled the teapot. "Well, I have a lot of work I plan to do on some cases I'm working on."

Rosie peered closer. "Your face is looking better," she said. "How does it feel?"

Mary ran her hand over her cheek. "A little tender. But good for the most part."

The doorbell rang again and Mary jumped.

"Well, aren't you a busy lady," Rosie said, turning in her seat and watching Mary answer the door.

Mary had barely opened the door, when it was pushed forward and Stanley strode into her house.

"I get a knock on the door at the ungodly hour of eight o'clock on a Sunday morning and a police officer is handing me the keys to old Betsey," he growled. "He wasn't old enough to shave, much less drive her.

"Then he tells me that someone tried to shoot you yesterday and then someone broke into your house. And you didn't call me to come over and help!"

"Mary, someone shot at you?" Rosie exclaimed, slipping off the stool and walking over. "Why didn't you tell us?"

"It was late... I was overwhelmed... I..."

The back door opened. "Mary, I just thought I'd sneak back in this way, so no one would see..." Bradley paused when he saw Rosie and Stanley staring at him, openmouthed.

"Rosie, Stanley, I believe you've met the police chief," Mary choked.

"Well, damn," the other three said simultaneously.

Chapter Thirty-one

"So, what you're saying is, you think this guy is targeting Mary because of the case she's working on?" Stanley asked, pointing the remainder of his cinnamon roll at Bradley from across the dining room table.

Mary leaned over and pressed the answering machine that was now sitting on her kitchen table and replayed the message from the night before. "He didn't just threaten – he followed through," Mary said.

"Mary," Rosie gasped. "I had no idea it was this dangerous."

Stanley nodded. "What do you need us to do?"

"Sorry, this isn't my usual kind of investigation," she explained. "I can't risk having either you or Rosie getting hurt."

Stanley turned and pointed his cinnamon roll at Mary. "Listen girlie, I've dealt with trickier situations than this," Stanley said. "I don't expect you to hand me a gun, but I do expect you to let me help."

Mary shook her head and was about to protest when Bradley interrupted. "Do either of you remember hearing about Jessica Whittaker's disappearance?" Bradley asked.

"Yes, I remember," Rosie said, nodding. "I remember because it was the same day Renee Peterson drowned."

"You knew Renee Peterson?" Mary asked.

"Yes, she worked for me when I had the boutique," Rosie explained. "It was while she was in high school."

"I remember her, cute girl, bright as a button," Stanley added. "Her death was such a shame."

"Did you ever talk to her about her work with the senator?" Mary said.

Rosie smiled. "Yes, she'd stop by the store whenever there was a big event. I'd help her pick out the right outfit. Matter of fact, the dress she wore that night was one from my shop. It almost made her late to the party and the senator was pretty frantic."

"How did you know that?" Mary asked.

"She had one of those fancy car phones, the senator had given it to her," Rosie explained. "My shipment was late and we were in the backroom making final alterations when I hear this ringing sound. She pulls this giant portable phone out of her bag – but she can't understand him because there was no such thing as cell coverage in Freeport back then.

"So she called him back on the store phone," Rosie continued. "He said no one from the campaign staff had arrived yet and asked her to hurry. She teased him that no one wanted to be around a sinking ship.

"She was so happy – she was glowing. That was the last time I saw her," Rosie sighed and shook her head.

"I always wondered about her death," Rosie added. "She had been on the high school swim team. It didn't make sense that she would drown. And I don't think the coroner's report showed that much alcohol in her system."

"They did a toxicology screen on her?" Bradley asked.

"Her mother told me they did it routinely in those kinds of situations," Rosie replied. "They made them hold off on the funeral for a couple of extra days in order to perform it."

Mary laid her hand on Rosie's. "I'm sorry, that must have been hard."

"Well, at least her parents know it was an accident," Rosie said. "Not like those little girls you're helping. It would be horrible to not know after all these years."

"Yes, it would be horrible," Bradley agreed.

Mary glanced at him. There was something in his voice that made her feel his comment was more than commonplace. She studied his face – his demeanor was very professional, but she could see the pain in his eyes.

Rosie and Stanley left soon after, promising not to mention their conversation to anyone else.

"Can they keep confidences?" Bradley asked.

"Well, they both love juicy gossip and Stanley loves to tease," Mary said with a smile. "But if they believe a slip of their lips is going to endanger me – they'll be silent."

"They're good friends, you're lucky," Bradley said.

Mary nodded. "Yes, they took me under their wings as soon as I moved to Freeport. I don't know what I would have done without them."

Bradley grinned. "I have a feeling you would have managed somehow."

Mary chuckled. "Maybe, but it wouldn't have been as much fun."

Mary grabbed a couple diet colas and handed one to Bradley before she sat down in front of her computer.

"I've run criminal checks on the campaign staff members, and except for a couple of speeding tickets, they're all clean," Mary said. "I've also run preliminary checks on all of the other guests. Nothing stands out."

"Well, just because they don't have a criminal record doesn't mean they can't be our guy," Bradley said. "Most serial killers were considered up-standing law abiding citizens before they were caught."

"So, we have two cases, two unique cases," Mary said. "One case involves the murder of one person, Renee, and another case involves the serial murders of at least five little girls, right?"

"Well, let me play devil's advocate," Bradley said. "What if they are connected? What if this is not just a big coincidence?"

"Yeah," Mary agreed, "there are no such things as coincidences."

"Right, so what do these cases have in common?"

Mary pulled out the files that listed the disappearances of the little girls.

"Okay, we have five deaths – if we count Jessica in the batch," she said. "The dates of the disappearances are July 6th, August 6th, September 6th and October 6th. Election day that year was on November 6th."

"So our killer's cool-off period was about thirty days," he said.

"It could mean that he couldn't have been Renee's killer because he had already killed Jessica."

"Yes," Bradley agreed.

"Or it could mean that he killed Renee for another reason, because she doesn't fit his usual profile," she added.

"Well, let's see what else we find that might connect the two cases," Bradley suggested, pulling half of the pile of papers toward him.

They worked quietly, examining each document carefully. After an hour Bradley got up and walked out to the kitchen. Mary stretched and looked over.

"I promised chili," he said, "and I'm a man of my word."

Mary smiled. "Are you sure? We could always just make sandwiches."

He cocked his eyebrow at her. "Are you, perhaps, disparaging my cooking abilities?" he asked.

"No. Never. Perish the thought," she laughed. "I'll keep reading if you don't mind."

"Be my guest."

The homey kitchen sounds in the background were calming as Mary read the files and tried to get her mind around someone who could indiscriminately take the lives of those innocent children. She couldn't get the picture of the little girls out of her mind. She knew they saved her life and the least she could do is help them move on.

She picked up the folder with the information about the children and flipped through the files until she found the child she was looking for. The little girl who had placed her hand on Mary's arm was Lillian Johnson and she was from Gratiot, Wisconsin, just on the other side of the Illinois state line. Her parents had called her their little Lily. She had two siblings, both younger and she had been a little mom to both of them. Her parents' statement said she would have never left her five-year-old brother and three-year-old sister alone in the backyard. She must have been forcibly removed. She disappeared on August 6, 1984.

Knowing her emotions might cloud her perception, Mary swapped that folder for the one with the senator's information. She flipped through his campaign itinerary until a date caught her eye.

"Wait a minute," she said aloud.

"What is it?" Bradley stopped chopping peppers and walked over to where Mary was pushing through the papers, trying to find her legal pad.

"The dates, the dates that the girls ended up missing. What were they?" she asked.

"July 6th, August 6th, September 6th, October 6th and finally, November 6th," Bradley said. "Why?"

"Look at this," Mary said, pointing to the itinerary. "August 6, 1984 – speaking engagement in Warren, Illinois – less than ten miles from Gratiot, where Lily was taken."

"And all of the other dates – all of the other months – speaking engagements in neighboring towns," she said, pulling out the rest of the files and comparing them.

"It all leads us back to one man," Bradley said.

"The senator," Mary supplied.

Chapter Thirty-two

The coroner's office was just a little bit larger than a closet and was housed in a corner of the lower level at the County Courthouse. The current coroner was actually one of the local funeral directors and rarely used his county office, but did most of his work from his mortuary. So, the office itself was just row upon row of file cabinets packed side by side in the small dim room.

Next to the coroner's office was the county clerk's office, a large spacious area encompassing the rest of the lower level of the courthouse. It consisted of an open area with a counter that separated the clerks from the general public and six offices with glass walls that surrounded the open area.

Mary waved to the county clerk as she entered the building and walked over to the counter to meet her. "Hi, Linda, happy Monday," she said.

The trim, dark-haired middle-aged woman groaned, "I need a weekend to recover from the weekend. What can I do for you?"

"I need to have some records pulled from the coroner's office – a file that's more than twenty-four years old. Do you know how I can get access to it?"

Linda Lincoln knew everything there was to know about Stephenson County. Mary had learned that Linda could have run the entire county single-handedly, but the entire county could not have run without Linda.

"Which file?" Linda asked.

"The autopsy report on Renee Peterson," Mary replied.

"Why, isn't that the strangest thing," she said slowly. "That file was taken from the courthouse last week. A junior clerk noticed the file drawer was open and saw that the folder was empty."

Mary's stomach dropped. Now what was she going to do?

"You'd think that someone didn't want you to have that file, Mary," Linda continued. "But fortunately for you, I know that the coroner at that time had a real bad habit of losing files, so we always made duplicates of everything. I'm sure it's in the vault. Why don't we take a little walk together?"

Mary grinned as Linda grabbed her keys and made her way around the counter. "Have I mentioned lately how much I admire your style?" Mary asked.

Linda laughed. "You just always got to be one step ahead of the crooks, honey," she said, "and then you've got it made."

They walked to the end of the hall and stopped in front of a solid steel door. Linda inserted the key, turned the lock and pushed it open.

The vault was actually a large room surrounded by reinforced steel to protect all of the county's records in case of fire. It had steel file cabinets standing side by side in aisles that were only about three feet apart.

"It gets a little tight in here," Linda said as she walked down the third aisle. "But it's as solid as Fort Knox."

Linda found the correct cabinet and pulled open the drawer. She ruffled through the folders and finally pulled one out.

"Here you are, Renee Peterson, autopsy performed on November 7, 1984," she said. "Do you need the whole file or just a part?"

"I'd like to look at the whole thing if I can," Mary said, "but I'm mostly interested in the toxicology report."

"Sure," Linda said, with a wink. "Why don't we just run back to my office and I'll make you a copy of everything. Then, when you return it, we can file it where the other one used to be."

"Thanks, Linda," Mary said. "You are a life saver."

It always amazed Mary at the way little things like phone numbers seemed to stick in your memory, even after not using them for years. Once back at her office, she dialed the number that she had used weekly when she was a Chicago cop.

"Cook County Coroner, Wojchichowski," the voice on the other end answered.

"Hey, Bernie, it's Mary O'Reilly," she said.

"Hey, little O'Reilly, how ya doing?"

Mary smiled. "I'm doing well," she replied, "although they don't have any good Polish food in Freeport."

"No kidding?" he said. "What kind of uncivilized place did you move to anyway?"

"I moved to Mayberry," Mary said.

"You know, Aunt Bea was Polish," Bernie said.

Mary laughed. "Yeah, I heard that."

Bernie chuckled. "So, what can I do for you?"

"I've got a tox report I'd like you to look over, if you wouldn't mind," she said. "It's almost twenty-five years old."

"Yeah, I was around back then," he chuckled. "Sure fax it on over. I'll take a look and call you back."

"Thanks, Bernie, you're the best," she said.

"Well, kochanie, it's because I'm Polish."

"Are you swearing at me in Polish again?" Mary teased, knowing that kochanie meant sweetheart.

Bernie laughed. "Look it up, kochanie, look it up."

"Bernie, thanks for doing this," she replied.

"Hey, no problem," Bernie said. "By the way, Mary, I got this nephew, nice kid, owns a bunch of apartment buildings. Want I should set the two of you up for a blind date?"

"Bernie, Bernie," Mary called into the phone while slapping her hand against the mouthpiece. "There seems to be something wrong with our connection."

Bernie laughed. "Yeah, just fax the report and we'll talk."

"Thanks, Bernie."

After she faxed the report, she sat down at her desk and dialed another familiar number. She leaned back in her chair and propped her feet up on the corner of her desk.

"Hi, Dad, how are you doing?" she asked when her father picked up the phone.

She could picture her dad sitting at the kitchen table in their spic and span kitchen. His blue eyes would be sparkling and there would be a smile on his face. He'd sit back in his chair and, if her mother wasn't home, prop his feet up on the chair next to him.

"Hey, Mary-Mary, how is life in the country?" he asked. "How's the ghost-busting business?"

"It's good," she said, running her hand over her cheek. "I had a run-in with a fort the other day – but I'm doing much better now."

His deep chuckle cheered her. "I remember the time we were all downtown looking at the Christmas lights on State Street and you walked into a street sign," he said. "As I recall, they had to replace the sign. So, did the fort come out better than the sign?"

"Oh, no, they had to call in some contractors to repair the damage," she said. "Ma always said I had your hard head – I guess she was right."

"So, what happened?" he asked.

"Well, if you must know, I was chasing a ghost," she said. "Funny thing, the ghost had no problem running through the fort."

"Mary, I hate to point this out, but ghosts don't have bodies, lassie, they can do things like that."

She laughed out loud. "I'll try to remember that, Dad," she said. "In my line of work, that'll be helpful."

"Are you sassing me, little lady?" he asked. Mary could picture his bushy eyebrows lifting.

She laughed again. "Oh, no, Dad," she said. "You'd never hear a word of disrespect from these lips. That would be Sean or Thomas, not your sweet Mary."

Chapter Thirty-three

Bradley stood quietly in the doorway, listening to Mary's side of the conversation. He didn't want to interrupt her time with her dad. But as he listened to her side of the phone call, he couldn't help but smile.

"No, Dad, everything's fine," she said. "I'm working on a great case. I'll tell you about it next time we're together.

"Yes, I know, Thanksgiving's just around the corner. I can't wait."

She paused and Bradley heard the soft sigh.

"I just wanted you to know that I love you," she said softly. "You've always been the best dad a girl could have.

"Okay, I will. Tell Ma that I love her too. I'll try and call when she has a day off.

"Bye, Dad."

She slipped her feet off the desk, carefully replaced the handset and rested her head in her hands.

She's worried, Bradley thought, disappointed in himself that he hadn't noticed it before. That was a goodbye call.

"You are not going to die...again," Bradley said.

Mary jumped. "Damn it, Bradley, would you please stop doing that to me. If I don't get shot, I'm going to die of a heart attack."

"You are not going to get shot," he said. "You're too smart for that."

He motioned toward the door. "And since I've got a little extra time," he said, "how about I turn your nice quiet door into an annoyingly squeaky one?"

"That would be great," she said.

"It won't be as much fun as scaring you," he said, "but for you, anything."

She smiled. "Thanks a lot."

He walked over, sat in the chair on the other side of the desk and put the bag on the floor. "Your dad?" he asked.

She smiled. "Yes, my dad," she said. "Monday is his day off."

"So, what's got you spooked?"

"Well, other than being shot at twice and having someone break into my house?" she asked.

He nodded.

"I went to the coroner's office this morning," she said. "The original report from Renee Peterson's autopsy was taken from the original file."

"What?" Bradley sat forward. "Who took it?"

Mary shrugged. "No one knows, but obviously someone who has more access than the average citizen," she replied. "I was lucky that Linda Lincoln, who is amazing by the way, knew where a copy of the report was stored. I just faxed it to an old friend at the Cook County coroner's office for a review and he'll be calling me back soon with his take on it."

"And you're spooked because..." he prompted.

"Because this guy seems to be either just on our heels or one step ahead of us," she said.

"When did the file go missing?" Bradley asked.

"Linda noticed it last week," she said.

"Well, then we are the ones doing the chasing," he said. "Shoe's on the other foot."

"What do you mean?"

"The perp finds out that you are accessing the files about either Renee or Jessica and gets spooked, right?"

Mary nodded.

"So he starts cleaning things up. He gets the old file out of the county building, he goes back to the fort, he goes back to the paper the night you're visiting with Anna," Bradley said. "But you are always there – either before he gets there or soon after. You're the one with the upper hand, not him. You have him spooked."

Mary thought about it for a moment and then grinned. "I really like your perspective much better," she said.

"Well, okay, better perspective, but actually a more risky one," he said. "He's the hunter being hunted."

"Which makes him more dangerous," Mary agreed.

"Yes, if he feels we're getting closer, he might do something desperate. So we just have to be on our toes all the time."

The ringing phone interrupted their conversation. From the caller ID, Mary saw that it was Bernie. She clicked on the speaker phone.

"Hi, Bernie, thanks for getting back to me so quickly," she said. "I've put you on speaker phone so my partner on this case, Police Chief Bradley Alden, can hear the information too."

"Okay, Mary, that's fine with me," he said. "So, the tox report is pretty normal, she had a little champagne that night and a couple of Tylenols. But I was a little surprised when I saw that they found traces of cyclohexanone hydrochloride in her system."

"What's that?"

"Well, its compound name is Ketamine," Bernie said. "It's a drug primarily used for general anesthesia, usually combined with some other drug. But in the 1980s it was the precursor of Rohypnol."

"You mean like roofies – the date rape drug?" Mary asked.

"Yes, perps liked using it because it reacted quickly, especially when it was injected. The results were a lack of inhibition and relaxation of voluntary muscles."

"So the victims seemed willing, even if they weren't," Mary said.

"Yes, it also caused the lasting anterograde amnesia," Bernie said. "The vics can't remember anything that happened while under the influence of the drug."

"So, why isn't it used anymore?" Bradley asked.

"Mostly because the newer drugs have a higher metabolization rate," Bernie explained. "By the time we get to the victim, the drug has already left their body or can give us false positives when we test. So you got no evidence."

"So how easy was it to get Ketamine?" Mary asked. "Would you need a prescription?"

"Depends, mostly on where you live," Bernie replied. "It's used widely for veterinary use; a farmer might be able to get his hands on it, especially back then."

"If you used it on children, weighing fifty to sixty pounds, how long would it take for them to react?" Mary asked.

"Well, depends on where you injected it," Bernie replied, "but it could take effect in a matter of minutes. For sure they would be groggy pretty quickly. Easy to manipulate."

"Makes sense," Bradley said. "One of the reports said that the victim would have never left the backyard. If she was disoriented, it would have been easy."

"How much Ketamine do you need to feel the effects?" Bradley asked.

"Well, for an adult a dose of 100 mg is usually enough to get them under the influence," Bernie said, "and for the size of child you're talking about, I'd say half of that."

"I'm trying to visualize what 100 mg is," Mary said.

"Well, 100 mg is about one-fiftieth of a teaspoon, and you'd need half of that," Bernie said. "It'd be like a TB test injection."

"So a pin prick covered with Ketamine could do it?" Bradley asked.

"Yes, it could," Bernie said.

"What if you use the same amount on an adult?" Mary asked.

"You get someone acting a little tipsy, slightly disoriented," Bernie said. "If they already had some alcohol in their system, like the victim in the tox report, it would be enough to be able to hold her under the water and drown her without too much trouble."

"Damn," Bradley said.

"Yeah, I agree with you, Chief," Bernie added.

"Bernie, thank you so much, you've really helped us," Mary said.

"Hope you get the creep," Bernie said.

"We will," Bradley responded immediately.

"So, Mary, about me setting you up with my nephew," Bernie began.

Bradley looked across at Mary, raised an eyebrow and grinned.

"Bernie, Bernie, what's that?" Mary asked, grabbing a piece of note paper and crunching it in front of the microphone. "That's what happens in small towns, can't count on the reception. Bernie? Bernie?"

"I ain't giving up, Mary," he yelled. "Not 'til you're married."

"Love you, Bernie," she called, just before disconnecting him.

"So, you want to get married?" she asked Bradley flippantly.

"Sorry, I already am."

Chapter Thirty-four

Mary sat in her living room staring at the flames flickering in the fireplace. She knew outside the house, in the driveway, was a marked police car and a uniformed officer. Inside all of the windows had been checked and double checked. She felt secure. Well, she reasoned, as secure as one can feel after being shot at and stalked for several days in a row. But she felt unsettled.

She placed her laptop on the couch next to her and lifted a large mug of spiced tea to her lips, then put it down. She pulled her stocking feet up so they were snugly tucked beneath her soft, fluffy robe and sighed deeply.

Bradley's comment about being married had left her feeling a little unsettled. *He's married,* she thought, *he doesn't look married.* She grinned. *Okay Mary, what does married look like?*

She threaded her fingers through her hair. *Face it,* she thought, *I'm feeling guilty because I had lustful thoughts about a married man.*

But, really, she argued with herself, *he could have told me from the beginning that he was married, so I could have taken him off the radar. What kind of married guy goes jogging around the park early in the morning looking like...?* She tried to come up with the correct descriptor, picturing his unshaven face, his teasing eyes, his toned muscles, his... *Okay, stop, Mary, he's married, you don't think about a married man's buns. But he really has a nice...body. Yes, a nice body. He's a good specimen of manhood.*

Damn.

She picked up her tea and took a sip. She really needed to get back to the case. That was much more productive. She took a deep breath and closed her eyes. That's when she heard it. Sobbing. Insistent sobbing.

She set her mug down and walked toward the sound. It was a little louder in the kitchen. She walked to the basement door; yes, it was coming from the basement. "Crap," she muttered, "if my basement has one of those portals to hell, I'm going after my real estate agent. That should have been disclosed."

She opened the door and paused. She wasn't working alone anymore. She had a partner. Besides, she'd seen all of those movies when the girl goes down the stairs because she hears a noise. She always ended up getting killed. Mary had been disgusted at the stupidity of the actress on the television screen, so she certainly wasn't going to take any extra risks in real life.

She pulled her cell phone out of her pocket and called Bradley. He answered on the first ring.

"What's wrong?"

She could hear panic in his voice and decided it was nice to have a partner that worried about you.

"I'm hearing some sounds coming from my basement. Someone is crying down there," she said, "but I decided to call you before I investigate."

"I'll be there in five minutes," he said. "Don't go down there alone."

"Yeah, I've seen the movies too," she said.

He chuckled. "Exactly. Five minutes."

She hung up the phone and headed upstairs to her room, deciding that five minutes would give her enough time to change into some ghost-following clothes.

He made it in less than four minutes and Mary had already changed into jeans and a sweatshirt. Bradley was dressed similarly.

"Let's go," she said simply and led him to the basement door.

"We don't have to keep the lights off?" he asked. At her puzzled glance he added, "You know, when you think there are ghosts in your room you turn on the light because it chases them away."

She nodded in understanding. "No, the lights being off only make it easier to see them," she said, "but the lights in my basement are dim enough that I should be able to see the ghost, if he wants to be seen."

She flipped on the lights and walked slowly down the stairs. The few scattered bare bulbs hanging from the ceiling threw shadows all around the room, making it difficult for Mary to discern anything out of the ordinary.

Mary stopped at the bottom stair and looked to her left. Tall shelves stood against unfinished concrete walls. There was nothing out of the ordinary there.

Then she peeked around at the underside of the staircase. In her childhood she had always been sure that something was lurking under the basement stairs, it just made sense to check there, just in case.

"Anything?" Bradley whispered.

Mary shook her head.

Her old furnace was in the center of the room, its stainless steel ducts branching out across the space, neatly blocking her view to the back of the basement. They passed the furnace. She glanced around the rest of the space. There was a hot water heater in one corner and some boxes filled with Christmas decorations and some unused furniture in the other corner. The only place she couldn't see was the workroom.

The pegboard covered door stood open. The space inside was dark, but Mary could picture it in her mind. A homemade workbench with a pegboard above it filled with tools. Next to the workbench were several tall shelving units filled with paint cans and other miscellaneous supplies. And spiders.

Mary really hated spiders. What self-respecting ghost would hide in a work room filled with spiders?

Then she heard it again, quiet sobbing coming from the corner with the workbench. *Crap!* She turned to let Bradley know. He was still looking around the room.

"You can't hear it, can you?" she asked.

He shook his head. "No, nothing," he said.

She sighed and patted him on the arm. "It's okay."

Bradley grabbed her hand and placed it back on his arm. "Wait."

He stopped and turned in the direction of the workroom too. He looked at her in amazement.

"I can hear it," he said.

"So when you touch me, you can hear it?" Mary asked.

He nodded and put his hand on her shoulder. "Lead on, Macduff."

They followed the noise and found their ghost. He was sitting on a stool next to the bench, his body bent, his head resting on his hands, crying. He was a tall man; slim, athletic, with blonde hair and casual attire. Mary thought she might know him.

"Excuse me," she whispered.

He looked up. She had missed the rope strung around his neck, but it was quite apparent now. And from the dark marks around his neck, it had been the cause of death. His face was pallid, contorted in a grisly mask of pain and angled to one side.

That had to have hurt.

"I'm dead, aren't I?" he asked sadly.

Mary nodded. She glanced over at Bradley who was staring at the apparition in shock. "You okay, Bradley?"

He nodded slowly.

She turned back to the ghost. "Yes, as far as I can see, you are dead," she answered. "Did you commit suicide?"

"No!" the ghost shouted, rising from the stool. "I did not commit suicide, but he...he made it look like I did."

"Who did it?" Mary asked.

The ghost paused, searching for the memory. "I don't know," he whispered, his anguish etched on his tortured face. "I can't remember."

"Can you remember your name?" Bradley asked, his law enforcement training overcoming his initial shock.

The ghost nodded. "Yes, but aren't you the Chief of Police?" he asked nervously. "I don't want the police involved in this. I can't have things get messy."

"Begging your pardon," Mary said, "but if it looks like you committed suicide, it's going to get messy."

The ghost sighed. "You're right, of course, I'm just not thinking straight. My name is Michael Strong," he said. "I'm President of the Freeport State Bank."

"Well, this is a first for me," Bradley said, running his hand through his hair as he leaned against Mary's kitchen counter. "How do you report a murder without knowing where the body is and having no report of a missing person?"

They had interviewed Mike for an hour and got nowhere. Finally they decided to take a break and come upstairs.

Mary brought Bradley a mug of tea, then sat at the kitchen table and sipped at her own. "So, what should we do next?" she asked.

He brought his tea to the table and sat across from her. "We try to get him to tell us where he was last night and see if anyone remembers anything," he said, "and we keep questioning him to see if he can remember anything about his death.

"This is so weird," he sighed.

"Welcome to my world," Mary said.

He looked over the table at her and smiled. "More like, welcome to 'The Twilight Zone.'"

"Like I said, welcome to my world."

"Why did he come here?" Bradley asked.

"I don't exactly know," Mary said, "It has something to do with my ability to communicate with them. They are drawn to me."

Mary leaned back in her chair and stretched, she glanced at the clock – it was after midnight. No wonder she was tired. But Bradley seemed energized, excited about the new world that had opened up to him. "Is it usual for ghosts to forget the circumstances behind their death?" he asked.

Mary shook her head. "No, actually, that's usually the event they remember the best," she paused, and then sat up in her chair. "But not if they were drugged."

"What do you mean?"

"So Mike Strong was part of the senator's campaign team," she said. "He was one of the few suspects in the death of Renee and now the little girls. How convenient of him to commit suicide and confess to all of the murders."

"I didn't commit suicide," the ghost screamed, materializing between them at the kitchen table.

Mary jumped back. Bradley looked at her. "What happened?" he asked.

"The ghost is back," she said, taking a deep breath. "And he reappeared somewhat unexpectedly."

He scooted his chair closer and took hold of her hand. "Okay, I see him now."

Mary turned her attention to the ghost. "I didn't think you committed suicide," Mary explained, after she caught her breath. "I just said that you might have been set up."

"Who would set me up?" he asked.

"Someone who doesn't want to be convicted of murder," she said. "Did you meet with someone last night?"

Mike shook his head. "No. I mean yes. But he wouldn't have done this," he said. "Besides, I was supposed to meet him at his office. I never made it there. It wasn't him."

"Why don't you tell us his name so we can be sure he didn't do this to you?" Bradley suggested.

"Because he is my friend and it was confidential," Mike said firmly. "He promised that he

226

wouldn't spill my secret. If I tell you, he'll tell everyone."

"Does it matter?" Mary asked. "If you're dead, does it really matter?"

Mike nodded and started to fade away. "It's my legacy," he said. "It's all I have left."

Chapter Thirty-five

Mary pulled up the drive at the Ryerson's house while the sun was just rising. She had called them on her way from Freeport to be sure they were both home and waiting. She grabbed the file and jogged up the stairs to the front door.

The door opened before she had a chance to knock. Joseph stood in the doorway. "Mary, you got here in record time," he said. "How can we help you?"

He directed her to the sitting room where Susan was waiting. Mary sat down across from Susan and pulled the photos of the little girls out and laid them on the table.

Joseph sat next to Susan and they both studied the photos. "I don't understand," Susan said. "How are these little girls related to our case?"

Mary turned to Joseph. "Do any of these girls look familiar to you, Senator?"

Joseph studied them and shook his head. "No, they don't. Should they?"

Mary allowed the photos to remain on the coffee table, staring up at the couple. "Each of these little girls was reported missing about twenty-four years ago, during the time of your campaign, senator," she said. "The girls lived in towns less than twenty miles from where you had made campaign stops. They each disappeared on the day you spoke at a town near them."

Susan gasped. "Surely, you don't think that Joseph…"

Mary pulled Jessica's photo out of the file and laid it next to the other ones. "Does this child look familiar?" she interrupted Susan.

Joseph nodded. "Yes, that's the little girl who was reported missing the same day Renee died," he said. "She was from Elizabeth."

Mary nodded. "I have reason to believe that whoever kidnapped the first four girls also took Jessica," she said.

Susan picked up the photos and examined each one. "They all look very much alike," she said, "except for Jessica."

Mary nodded. "Yes, they could have been sisters."

Susan put the photos down and looked across at Mary. "You know that Joseph couldn't have done this, don't you?"

Mary nodded. "Yes, he was at the house waiting for election returns," she said. "The media was probably parked right outside your house all day. It would have been impossible for him to have driven to Elizabeth without being noticed."

Joseph moved the photos around on the table. "But there is too much correlation between the snatchings and my campaign to make this all a coincidence," he said. "Someone in my campaign is responsible."

Mary nodded. "That's what it looks like. I need you to help me decide who it could be."

Mary pulled out her legal pad and pen. "What can you tell me about Jerry Wiley?"

Susan laughed. "No, not Jerry," she said. "First, he was never on the campaign trail with us because we never knew what he was going to say or..."

She stopped, bit her lip and glanced at her husband. He nodded at her.

"We didn't know what condition he would be in," she finished.

"You mean you didn't know if he would be stoned or not?" Mary asked.

They both looked surprised. "Jerry told me about that habit when I interviewed him earlier," she said.

"How about Mike Strong?" she asked.

Susan shook her head. "Well, Mike wouldn't be interested in little girls," she blurted out, then stopped.

Joseph turned to her, confused. "Why not?"

Susan hesitated. "Because he wasn't interested in girls," she said pointedly.

"What?" Joseph asked. "I don't understand."

Susan sighed. "Mike Strong is gay," she said.

"What? Are you sure?" Joseph exclaimed. "He's married."

"So?" Susan responded. "Gay men who don't want people to know about their preferences often marry. Besides, being who he was, he had a lot of expectations to live up to. His parents would have disowned him if they found out."

"But, but how did you know?" he asked.

She shrugged. "We spent a lot of time together, talked about a lot of things. We became friends and late one night after quite a few beers, he told me. He swore me to secrecy, but I think under the circumstances, he'd be okay with my telling his secret."

Mary thought about the poor tortured ghost in her basement and finally understood his reluctance to talk, even in death.

Mary nodded. "I promise you that his secret will remain confidential," she said.

"But that doesn't rule him out, does it?" Joseph said. "Being gay doesn't necessarily mean he couldn't be a serial killer."

"You're right," Mary said, "I'm not ruling out any possibilities."

"So, that leaves Hank Montague," Joseph said, leaning back against the couch. "I think you are batting three strikes here. Hank is well-respected and well-known. I think if he were a serial killer we would have figured it out long before now."

"I don't think I would consider him well-liked," Susan said, and then she added, "Not that I think he's a murderer, he's just a pig."

Joseph was surprised. "What? I never knew you felt that way about him," he said.

"Well, you were busy campaigning, so I had to deal with some of the little details," she said. "His condescending manner to women had me putting out little fires all over the area. I think he believed he was more important than the candidate. Even on the night of the election party, he did it again."

Mary was immediately intrigued. "Susan, what do you mean?"

"On the night of the party, Joe was going crazy because everyone was late," she said. "I was running interference, trying to entertain the media and get ready for the guests, and I was not pleased with the campaign staff.

"Finally, Renee and Mike arrived and I put them to work," she continued. "When I asked about Hank, Renee mentioned she had seen Hank on the side of the road near Tapley Woods, but he waved her on, so she didn't think he had car issues."

"He was parked near Tapley Woods?" Mary asked. "Do you remember the time?"

Susan shrugged. "The polls closed at seven p.m., but we were getting results in before that and it was looking good for Joe. I guess Renee and Mike got here at about six o'clock. But Hank didn't get here until six-thirty. I was really angry with him."

"Where was Jerry?" Mary asked.

"Oh, he got here early in the afternoon," Susan said, "but he had excused himself too many times to be of much help by the time the party started."

Mary nodded. So Jerry wasn't as discreet with his habit as he had thought. "When Hank finally arrived..." she prompted.

"He came walking in, really agitated," Susan said, remembering. "His clothes were a little messy; it almost looked like he had just thrown something on, not taken care with his appearance.

"I was going to comment about that when I happened to look down and saw that he tracked mud into the main hallway, just before all of the guests were supposed to arrive."

Mary thought back to day she followed Jessica. It had been sunny and dry.

"But it wasn't rainy the day of the election, was it," Mary said.

Susan nodded. "You're right," she said. "It was a beautiful Indian Summer day. He would have had to have been traipsing around the woods to get that muddy. Once again, he showed a complete lack of consideration for everyone else."

"What did he say when you questioned him?" Mary asked.

Susan shrugged. "He was so late, I decided to let it go until after the party, then I was going to give him a piece of my mind," she said. "But I guess it totally slipped my mind. I mean, a little mud seemed so unimportant compared to Renee's death. I guess we were all in shock for a while."

Mary nodded. "Yeah, that's understandable," she said. "Was there anyone else that could have been present at all of the campaign stops?"

Joseph thought about it for a moment. "Well, you know, anyone from the local media who covered politics would have been there," he said. "I also had

233

several groupies who were fairly devoted supporters and they came to just about every event."

"Do you still have their names?" Mary asked.

"Yeah, I'm sure I do," he said, "but it will take some digging."

"If you could e-mail them to me, I'd really appreciate it," she said.

Mary stood up and thanked them for their help. They walked her to the door. Mary opened the door, paused and turned back to them.

"I think I'm getting closer to finding the suspect," she said, "and whoever it is might be getting nervous and might act irrationally. So exercise extra precautions for the next little while. Be suspicious of everyone."

Joseph and Susan both nodded.

"Are you going to bring in the police?" Susan asked.

Mary nodded. "As soon as I have all the information I need, I'll bring law enforcement into the case," she said, "but I promise to be very discreet."

Susan reached out and took Mary's hand. "Thank you for all you've done. Be careful."

Mary smiled. "I will."

Chapter Thirty-six

It took Mary about fifteen minutes to drive from the Ryerson's home to Tapley Woods. She parked her car and walked to the edge of one of the trails. The air was cool and crisp and the sun was shining, a perfect fall day. The paths were still muddy from the rainstorms a few nights before and there were a couple small patches of ice where the sun didn't reach.

She took a deep breath and then exhaled, trying to clear her mind and focus on the case. She thought about Jessica and Renee. She pictured Renee driving to the Ryerson's, eager and excited about the party.

The angle of the sun changed and the day grew warmer. Mary turned when she heard the car horn. Renee Peterson, happy and excited, slowed down and pulled over to the road. "Do you need some help?" she called, then shrugged and pulled back onto the road and sped away.

Mary turned in the direction that Renee had been looking. She watched and waited for several moments. Then Jessica appeared before her. She was laying on her back, suspended in mid-air, her arms and legs hanging motionless toward the ground. She floated toward her. Mary watched, transfixed, as

Jessica came closer. Then the ghost moved through her and continued down the path.

Mary looked down and saw footprints appear in the path before her, just underneath Jessica's floating body. The vegetation was brushed to either side to make way for the unseen person who was carrying the little girl.

Mary kept her eyes on Jessica and noticed a slight movement of her head. She was still alive! Suddenly the abductor's pace increased. He knew it, he knew she was alive.

They traveled uphill on the trail for fifteen minutes and then he turned sharply to the left, off the trail and through heavy brush. Mary followed, beating back the branches and leaves that skimmed against her face.

The trees and bushes cleared to reveal a limestone ridge high above the surrounding countryside. Aware that the geology might have altered in twenty plus years, Mary kept a safe distance away from the ledge, but she could see from where she stood that the drop-off was more than forty feet. Mary turned back to Jessica's still body. He had brought her to the edge and held her there. He seemed to be waiting for something.

Jessica moved again. Her head lifted and her eyes fluttered open. She stared up at the face that only she could see.

"I want my mommy!" she cried.

But before she could say another word, Jessica's body was tossed off the cliff down to the woods below. Mary eyes filled with tears as she listened to the terrified scream. Then she heard the sound of Jessica's little body hitting the ground and the scream abruptly stopped. Mary dropped to her knees, wrapped her arms around herself and cried.

The air was growing cold and the sun was shining directly in her face when Mary stopped crying a few minutes later. She wiped the tears from her eyes, stood up and looked around. This was Jessica's final resting place. The area hadn't changed too much in twenty-four years.

She pulled out her cell phone. She needed to talk to Bradley and let him know what she'd discovered. Actually, she admitted to herself, she really just needed to hear a human voice. She dialed the number but nothing happened. She glanced at the bars, no service. Well, really, that was understandable.

"How did you find me?"

Mary jumped and spun around. Mike Strong's ghost stood a few feet away from her. However, when she looked through his translucent body, she could see the human remains of Mike Strong hanging only a few yards away, swinging from a tall oak tree at the edge of the ridge.

"I didn't know you were here," she said.

But it made perfect sense.

"Are you going to help me down?" he asked.

Mary looked at the stiffened and discolored body; it had already started to decompose. At that moment she was glad she was no longer a police officer. "I can't, Mike," she said. "I can't disturb the scene of the crime. But I will report it, so you can have a proper funeral."

"I didn't do it," he insisted. "I didn't commit suicide."

"I know that, Mike," she said. "I know that you were set up."

"I didn't kill that little girl," he said, crying. "I could never kill little girls. I have a little girl of my own."

"I know, Mike," she said. "You didn't do this, but we will find the person who did."

She could see that his emotional state was unstable and she hesitated to interview anyone in this condition, but if he could just tell her who he spoke to that night, she might be able to put all of the pieces together.

"Mike," she said softly. "I just came from seeing the Ryersons. You remember the Ryersons, don't you?"

Mike sniffled. "Yes, I do," he said. "Susan is one of the loveliest people I have ever met."

"Yes, she is," Mary agreed. "And she really cares about you. Mike, I want you to know that she told me about your secret, so you don't have to be…"

"What! She told you! How could she?" he screamed. "I trusted her! I trusted her! Oh, God. My family! My parents!"

He ran around the area, his hands on his head.

"No, no, no, no!" he screamed and then disappeared.

Chapter Thirty-seven

Hank Montague entered Bradley's office without knocking. Bradley looked up from his computer, surprised. "What can I...?"

"I just got a call from Mike Strong's wife, Wendy," he said. "Something's wrong. We need to get to their house immediately."

Bradley's initial reaction was relief. He had been trying to figure out how to work on a murder with no body and he was getting nowhere. "Did she mention what was wrong?" he asked, trying to act normal.

"No, but she sounded upset," Hank said, "We'll take my truck so we don't draw any undue attention to the situation. Mike wouldn't have wanted that."

Bradley grabbed his phone, his revolver, his handcuffs and his jacket and followed the mayor out of his office. "Dorothy, the mayor and I have a meeting," he said. "I'm not sure how long I'm going to be gone. You can reach me by phone."

Dorothy nodded and resumed her typing.

They used the back door of City Hall and climbed into Hank's pick-up. Bradley was a little surprised when Hank exited on to the highway rather than driving through town. "Where does Mike live?" he asked.

"Well, Wendy asked us to meet her out of town," Hank replied smoothly. "More privacy."

Bradley felt the hair on the back of his neck stand on end. There was something wrong with this situation. "How long have you known Mike?" Bradley asked, conversationally.

Hank shrugged and accelerated past a dairy truck. "For about thirty years now," he said. "We worked together several years ago."

"On Ryerson's campaign, right?"

Hank turned his head and a smile slowly crept over his face. "You are a bright young man, aren't you?" he said. "Yes, Mike and I worked together."

"When was the last time you saw Mike?" Bradley asked.

"Oh, I believe it was the other night," he said, stroking his fingers thoughtfully across his chin. "Yes, I believe it was Sunday night. Mike was supposed to meet me later in the evening. But he never showed up. I wonder what delayed him?"

"Did you call to find out?" Bradley asked.

Hank shook his head. "No, it was a favor I needed," he said, "and I really didn't want to push him."

Hank increased the truck's speed.

"You're going pretty fast," Bradley commented, watching the speedometer reach seventy-five miles per hour. "This road really wasn't meant to handle that kind of speed."

Hank shrugged. "Speed might discourage you from doing something stupid while I'm driving."

"And why would I want to do that?" Bradley asked.

"Because we both know you are not as incompetent as I had hoped when I hired you," he said. "Pity."

Bradley angled himself so his back was against the door. "Why would anyone want an incompetent police chief?"

Hank laughed. "It's so much easier to get away..." He paused and then turned and smiled at Bradley. "...with murder."

Hank jerked the steering wheel and the truck swerved. Instinctively Bradley reached over to straighten the wheel. Hank grabbed Bradley's arm. Bradley pulled back, but not before he felt the slight piercing in his forearm. "What the hell?" he shouted.

Hank's smile grew. "Don't worry, Chief," he said, "it won't kill you; it will just make you a little groggy. The killing part comes later."

Bradley felt his body react to the drug immediately. He slumped back against the seat. He concentrated on trying to stay awake.

"You probably didn't notice my ring," Hank said. "I had it specially made. It carries just enough drugs on the hidden tip to put an adult to sleep. It's really my favorite toy."

"You killed them...all those girls," Bradley said, his speech slurring.

"Why yes, I did," Hank agreed pleasantly. "But they were all willing to die. They wanted me, you see."

"So, you're not only a bastard…you're a sick bastard," Bradley said.

"Oh, no, I'm a highly intelligent person," he said. "Genius level, actually. That's why I have the right to use those of lesser intelligence for my pleasure."

"No one has that right," Bradley murmured.

Hank shook his head. "Oh, Chief, don't be naive," he said. "Cats are smarter than mice; coyotes smarter than rabbits; humans, for the most part, smarter than cows – kill or be killed. That's the way of the world."

"Preying on those…weaker…is not the way of the world," Bradley said, fighting the darkness that was enveloping him. "It's…it's just your…damn excuse to justify what you do."

"Such an idealist. It's too bad you won't be around to see what I have in mind for our Miss O'Reilly. You might have enjoyed it – I've seen the way you watch her," he said. "Such a lovely thing. She wants me too."

"No," Bradley groaned, he tried to lunge toward Hank but he couldn't move his body.

Bradley's phone rang in his shirt pocket. Hank pulled to the side of the road and retrieved it. "Well, well, our Miss O'Reilly is looking for you," he said. "What do you think she wants?"

Hank sat back and stroked his fingers across his chin again. "If she can't get you, she'll call Dorothy," he reasoned. "Dorothy will tell her that you left with me. Thank you for giving her that bit of information, Chief.

"And if I know our overachieving private investigator, she'll come looking for you," he said. "Perhaps we ought to help her find us."

Hank looked over his shoulder, did a quick U-turn and headed back to Freeport.

Chapter Thirty-eight

Why wasn't Bradley answering his phone?

Mary tried for the fourth time as she took the exit ramp into Freeport. "Damn it, Bradley, pick up."

Finally she called the non-emergency number. "Dorothy," she said, "this is Mary O'Reilly; do you know where Chief Alden is? I really need to get in touch with him."

Mary hung up her phone with growing trepidation. Dorothy's information that Bradley was with Hank did nothing to reassure her. Everything pointed to Hank Montague. Everything but solid evidence. She needed to find something to link Hank with the murders. Then she could call in the rest of the police force and find Bradley.

Mary pulled into a parking lot and flipped through the file she had brought to the Ryersons. Halfway through she found what she'd been looking for; the lists of names and addresses. She scanned the list; Hank Montague lived on Greenfield Rd, only a few minutes away.

She drove to the address and parked up the street between several other cars, hoping that her unique car wouldn't be immediately noticeable.

Jogging down the street, she looked around her, relieved to see that this neighborhood sat mostly empty during the day. She sprinted down Hank's driveway and followed the narrow sidewalk into his backyard.

The house was a split-level with patio doors at the ground level. The doors were partially concealed under a second level deck. Mary looked around for an appropriate tool and found a heavy stone near the border of the garden.

Picking up the stone she walked to the door, and when she confirmed that it was locked, she hefted the stone in her hand and smashed through one of the panels closest to the knob. She knocked the excess shards onto the ground and reached in and opened the door.

The lower level hadn't been finished. The walls were slate gray concrete and the floor, faded pink linoleum. Enough sunshine spilled in through the doors and the scattered basement windows that she didn't need to turn on the lights.

Her steps echoed in the room and she shivered. *This place feels creepy*, she thought. She looked around. There were several closed doors that she assumed led to the mechanics of the house and storage areas, but the rest of the room was empty. She headed toward the stairs in the far corner.

"He doesn't like it down here."

Mary gasped and spun around.

"I'm sorry, my dear. I didn't mean to frighten you," the woman said.

Mary had never been good at guessing ages, but she figured this woman had been about the age of her mother. She was dressed in what her mom had called a housedress, had rollers in her hair and slippers on her feet. *What cruel act of fate resigned her to spend the eternities dressed like that?* she wondered.

"Why doesn't he like it down here?" she asked.

The woman smiled slyly. "Because I'm down here," she said, "and he doesn't like it. He killed me, you know."

Mary shook her head. "No, I didn't know," she said. "I'm so sorry."

The woman shrugged. "Well, if anyone was to blame, it was me," she said easily. "He is my son after all."

"Is he trying to kill you?" she asked, with the same calm voice as one would use when asking about your choice for dessert.

"I think he might want to kill me," Mary revealed. "I know that he's killed quite a few people, and I would really like to stop him."

His mother nodded and folded her hands across her chest. "Yes, he's brought quite a few of them here to be killed," she said. "He is a disappointment to me.

"He reminds me quite a bit of his father," she confided. "Confidentially, I think he was nuts."

Mary could just imagine. She glanced around the room again.

"Can you show me where he might keep some things that I can use for evidence?" she asked.

"Are you an investigator?" the woman asked with delight.

Mary nodded.

"I love Perry Mason," the woman said. "You must be very smart."

Mary sighed. She really didn't have the time to coddle a chatty ghost, but if she could get her to help, she could possibly lead her quickly to some important evidence.

"Well, just like Perry, I often have to rely on helpful assistants," she said. "I would love for you to help me."

The woman preened. "Yes, I can be very helpful," she agreed. "Follow me. I'll show you where he keeps his treasures."

They walked up the stairs and entered the main living area. An office, bathroom and bedroom lay to the left and the living room and kitchen were on the right. "This way," his mother said. "He keeps things in his office."

The office was meticulously neat. The books on the shelves, Mary noted, were in alphabetical order. "He's a bit of a fanatic about order," his mother commented.

Mary moved behind the desk and tried to open the drawers. "Locked," she sighed.

"Oh, the key is in the file cabinet," his mother offered.

Mary searched the cabinet and found the key. She unlocked the desk and opened the top drawer. Inside she found a brown vial. She pulled it out.

"That's his poison," his mother said. "That's what he uses to drug his victims."

Mary put the vial on the top of the desk and continued to search. She pulled out a collection of odds and ends, including a pair of Strawberry Shortcake ribbons. Jessica had been wearing them the day she died.

"Those are his trophies," his mother said, leaning over the desk. "He has one of my curlers in there."

Suddenly, his mother straightened. "I hear his truck," she said. "He's home. Run!"

Mary heard the garage door open and knew it was too late. She looked at the vial. "Does he always drug his victims?" she asked.

Nodding, his mother sighed. "I think he likes to make his victims helpless."

Mary grabbed the vial and ran to the bathroom down the hall. She dumped the contents into the toilet, quickly rinsed the vial several times before filling it with water. She wiped it down, closed it and put it back in the drawer.

"He has more of it," his mother said, "in the closet."

"Well, let's hope that he is as compulsive as he appears," Mary said.

Mary locked the desk, put the key back in the file cabinet and hurried out of the room and back down the basement stairs.

"I wish I could help you, my dear," his mother said, "but he can see me when I'm here and he always says nasty things to me."

She disappeared into the shadows of the room. Mary turned and ran back to the patio doors. Just as she grasped the handle, she heard a gun being cocked behind her. She froze at the sound.

"Leaving so soon?" Hank asked. "I'm sure that Chief Alden and I will be sad to see you go."

Mary let go of the handle and turned back to Hank. "What have you done to Bradley?"

Chapter Thirty-nine

"Bradley, is it?" Hank laughed. "You fancy yourself attracted to him? He's still pining over his missing wife. You haven't got a chance with him. But you have a chance with me."

He moved closer and skimmed his hand across her lips, along her jaw and rested on her neck. She shivered with revulsion. "You're trembling because you want me," he whispered, slowly licking his lips.

"Like I want a kick in the head," she replied.

His hand tightened on her neck.

"Oh, yeah, strangling someone is so attractive," she whispered, his fingers stifling her breath. "I bet you get all the girls that way."

He growled, released his hold on her throat and sent her reeling with a powerful backhand to her cheek, knocking her to her knees.

"Don't play with me, little girl," he threatened, grabbing her by the hair. "You will not win."

He pulled her up to her feet and shook her. Mary clenched her teeth, pain reverberating deep in her scalp; but she was not going to let him see her pain.

He was angry, almost out of control. She noted the perspiration beading on his face and his accelerated breathing. Did she dare push him further to the edge?

"I met your mother," she said. "Lovely woman…or at least she was."

His eyes darted around the room. "You leave my mother out of this," he said.

"You killed your own mother," Mary continued. "What kind of a man are you?"

He released the grip on her hair. The hand that held the gun was shaking. He wiped his brow with the other hand.

"She made me do it," he whispered. "She made me kill her."

Mary snorted. "Yeah, just like the little girls," she said. "I saw them too, all of them. They're waiting for you."

"Shut up, bitch!" he yelled, slapping her again. "Just shut up!"

He grabbed her arm and pushed her across the room, the gun poking into her rib cage. "You can help me with your boyfriend and then I'll give you a closer encounter with your ghost friends."

He guided her through a door that led to the garage. The garage door was closed, the overhead lights were on and the pickup was in the center of the room. He pushed her forward. "Open the door," he ordered. "Slowly."

She inhaled quickly; she could see Bradley's motionless body through the window.

"He's not dead yet," Hank taunted. "He's just resting."

Mary opened the door carefully, leaning forward to compensate for Bradley's weight. She reached in and repositioned him, so he was resting against the seat instead of the door, and then opened the door the rest of the way.

"Good girl," Hank sneered. "Now move him."

Mary turned. "What?"

"I said move him," Hank repeated. "I need him in the back of the truck."

Mary knew that the only reason he wanted Bradley in the truck bed was to hide him as he transported him somewhere else. Were her chances better here or there?

"Are you nuts?" Mary asked, knowing full well the answer to that question. "He's more than twice my weight. I might drop him."

Hank shoved the gun into her rib cage. "Yeah, either that or I just put a bullet in his brain right now," he said, "and then you move him. I understand that dead weight is even heavier."

Mary decided not to risk pushing Hank. She didn't know if he was bluffing or not. She lifted Bradley's arm, placed it around her shoulder and then angled herself so her back was against his side. She grabbed his leg and pulled it forward, easing him out of the car into a fireman's carry.

"You're stronger than you look," Hank said.

He opened the gate and stepped back. "Put him in there," he said.

Mary struggled with Bradley's weight, but was able to carry him around the truck. She turned and backed into the bed area, squatting down until Bradley was lying on the steel floor. She turned and pushed him further in, so he was lying from the top to the bottom of the bed.

She took a deep breath and turned back to Hank.

"Get his handcuffs from his belt," he instructed. "And don't bother looking for his gun. The chief has already generously given it to me."

This can't be good, she thought. She glanced around the garage, hoping for another option, but with him standing less than four feet away with a gun pointed at her, her best choice was to obey. It only took her a few moments to locate the handcuffs. She reluctantly handed them to Hank.

"And the keys," he ordered.

Damn, she thought. She tossed him the keys.

"Now climb in," he said, motioning to the back of the truck.

Mary climbed in, sliding up next to the inert Bradley. "Oh, no," Hank said, moving closer. "We want you much cozier than that. Lay down."

Mary slid in next to Bradley. "Now, put your arms around him," Hank ordered.

She wrapped her arms around his neck. "Do you think I'm an idiot?" Hank snarled. "Wrap your arms around his waist."

No, not an idiot, Mary thought. *A lunatic, a jerk, a serial killer, yes, but unfortunately not an idiot.*

She squeezed one arm under Bradley's body and laid the other one over him. Hank leaned over the side of the bed and slapped the cuffs through a hook on the box and then over Mary's wrists. "This might keep you from trying to escape while I finish getting a few things together."

A few moments later, she heard a door close and knew that she only had a few minutes to think of a new plan.

Mary sighed, resting her head against Bradley. Yeah, there was nothing like being anchored to a two-hundred-pound police chief to keep you from making a quick escape. "Bradley," she whispered. "Bradley, can you hear me?"

Nothing.

"Well, crap," she muttered.

"Miss O'Reilly?"

Mary craned her head to look outside the truck. Mike Strong was standing in the garage. "I came to apologize," he said. "You were just trying to help me and I got carried away."

Mary shook her head. Damn, she had the strangest life.

"As you can see, Mike, I'm a bit busy right now," she said, "but I appreciate you taking the time to apologize."

Mike peered at them. "Is he going to kill you?"

Mary nodded. "I think that's the general idea," she said. "Oh, by the way, it was Hank who killed you. He drugged you so you wouldn't remember."

Mike's eyes widened and then narrowed. "He lied to me," he said. "He wanted me to take the blame."

Mary nodded. "Yes, and it looks like he's going to get his wish," she said, hoping to motivate him. "With Chief Alden and me out of the picture, no one will know the truth."

The ghost shook with rage and seemed to expand before Mary's eyes. No longer a victim, he stood straighter and his presence was more forceful. "There is no way my family is going to think I killed little girls," he said. "I'm going to stop him."

Then he deflated a little. "How?"

Just then they both heard Hank's approaching footsteps. Panic flashed on Mike's face and he disappeared.

"Well, that didn't last long," she muttered.

"Who are you taking to?" Hank snarled, looking down at her from the side of the truck.

"Some of the ghosts of the people you murdered," she said truthfully. "Don't you feel them? They're all around you."

He paled and glanced around. "If they were here, I'd see them," he spat.

Mary shrugged. "Not if they don't want you to see them," she said. "But they follow you. Everywhere you go, they follow you."

"I'm going to shut you up, bitch," he shouted as he poked his ring into Mary's arm. "And then I'm going to have a little fun with you."

He ran his hand along her arm, her shoulder, her neck and finally across her lips. "Oh, yes, lots of fun."

Mary shuddered.

"Really? With your mother watching?" Mary slurred her voice. "That's perverted."

Hank glanced around again. "She's not here," he said. "She not's here!"

"She wearing a house dress and has curlers in her hair," Mary said weakly. "She's watching you, Hank. Always watching you."

He looked around again nervously. Then he looked back at Mary, who pretended to be unconscious. "You're going to wish I had my fun here," he said. "Now I'm going to be sure that you're awake to enjoy it."

He pulled the vinyl bed cover over the top and fastened it down. Then he slammed the gate closed. Except for the light peeking in at the edge of the gate, Mary and Bradley lay in total darkness. She heard the engine start and the sound of the garage door opening. Moments later she felt him turn out of his driveway and head down the street.

Mary's arm felt slightly numb, but she hadn't really felt any other effects of the pin prick. She prayed that he had chosen the vial in the desk. She took a deep breath, so far so good.

The truck veered quickly around a corner and the motion caused Bradley to roll and nearly crush Mary. *Wouldn't that be ironic,* Mary thought, *crushed to death by Bradley.*

She levered her feet against the side of the bed and pushed her body against him, repositioning him so she could breathe.

"Thanks, Chief," she muttered, inhaling deeply. "Now to come up with a plan."

Chapter Forty

Mary knew that they were getting closer to Tapley Woods, but she hadn't come up with a plan yet. She hadn't really been able to get much past the first challenge – Bradley. Even if she could somehow escape from the handcuffs, there was no way she could carry him to safety. The five foot trek from the passenger's side to the truck bed nearly did her in.

Besides, she really hadn't had any luck getting the cuffs loose from the hook on the side of the bed. She had pulled on the steel hook to try and either break the hook or the cuff chain, but both had held.

She laid her head against Bradley's chest and sighed. She really didn't want to die again. And if she were going to die, she really wanted to take Hank with her.

Bradley inhaled deeply. Mary raised her head. "Bradley," she said, "are you awake?"

Bradley groaned. Loudly.

Mary wondered if Hank had the cab back window open. She certainly didn't want Hank to know that either of them was awake.

"Shhhh," she whispered.

Bradley groaned again. Mary kicked him in the leg. "Bradley, you need to be quiet," she said.

He continued to fight his way out of the drug, tossing his head and moaning. If she only had her hands free, she would have covered his mouth. She frantically looked around. Nothing.

"Damn," Mary decided, "there's only one thing to do. Sorry Mrs. Alden, wherever you are."

She slid up and placed her mouth over his. Mary could feel that he was startled at first, but after a moment, natural lust replaced confusion. Not only was he returning the kiss, he was doing it with gusto. Mary's head swam. Wow! He was good at this.

His lips slid off hers as he trailed a path of kisses across her face and along her neck. "Mary," he whispered softly. "Oh, Mary."

She was tingling from head to foot, as each new wave of excitement washed over her. "I sure hope your wife's name isn't Mary," she murmured, before his lips found her mouth again.

The truck hit a bump. Mary swore. "Crap! Someone is trying to kill us. What am I thinking?"

She pulled her head away. "Bradley, stop," she said in her firmest voice.

"Mary, please, just another kiss," he moaned, his arms stroking up her back.

"Bradley, stop," she said, as he nibbled on her chin and lower lip.

She sighed. "I'm sorry, Bradley, but I did ask," she said and then sunk her teeth into his bottom lip.

That did the trick. Bradley pulled back, bringing Mary along with him. His eyes were now open, wide, and he was staring at her as if he had just woken from a dream. "What happened?" he asked, his voice still slurred. "Did you just bite me?"

Mary nodded. "It seemed like the thing to do at the time," she replied.

He tried to move away and she came along with him. "Mary, why are you lying on my chest?" he asked.

"Because my arms are handcuffed behind your waist," she answered. "And you're actually cutting off the circulation to them right now."

"Oh, sorry," he said, shifting. "Better?"

She nodded. "Yes, thanks."

"Why didn't you use the keys?" he asked.

"Because I had to give them to Hank," she replied. "He's smarter than he looks."

"Did you give him the extra set?" he asked, still obviously befuddled.

"No, I didn't know you had an extra set," she said, trying to remain calm. "Perhaps you could give them to me."

Bradley cheerfully dug the keys out of his pocket and maneuvered around to unlock Mary's hands. "There, that's better," he said with a smile, and then he giggled.

This wasn't good. He was coming off the drug like a cheerful drunk. "Bradley," she said slowly. "I need you to concentrate. I need you to work past the fuzzy happy part of your brain and go to the warrior-police guy, okay?"

Bradley nodded and smiled. "Okay."

Mary wasn't convinced.

"My guess is that Hank is driving us to Tapley Woods," she said. "I think that last turn was the junction with Highway 84. So we only have a few minutes before we get there. We need to have an escape plan."

"I'll shoot him," Bradley offered helpfully.

"He has your gun," Mary replied.

"Oh, then that won't work."

Mary sighed. Somehow she didn't think that Bradley's warrior-police guy was coming back anytime soon.

"So, how do your legs feel?" she asked.

She felt a large hand squeeze her thigh.

"Bradley, that was my leg."

"Oh, sorry, but what a relief, I thought I had lost feeling in my legs."

Maybe death isn't all that bad, Mary thought.

Mary slid down to the bottom of the truck bed. She felt around in the darkness and located the interior latch. She felt Bradley move down beside her. "What did you find?" he asked.

Mary thought he seemed a little more rational. "The latch for the gate," she said. "Perhaps we can crawl out when he stops the truck."

"If he has my gun, we won't have a chance," he said, his voice sounding a little more serious.

Oh, thank goodness, Bradley's coming back.

"Well, he has to slow down once he enters the woods," Mary said. "We could roll out while the truck is still moving."

Bradley looked at her. "It's gonna hurt."

She smiled back at him. "Yes, but so does dying."

Chapter Forty-one

Mary could feel the minute they left regular pavement and turned onto the rough maintenance road. She turned to Bradley. He met her eyes and nodded. Yes, he was back.

She reached up, released the latch and slowly lowered the gate. The brown dirt road slipped past them quickly. The drop was only a couple of feet, but Bradley was right, it was going to hurt.

"Roll sideways," Bradley suggested. "And when you hit the road, keep rolling to your left so he doesn't see you through his side mirror."

Mary nodded, and shifted in the bed so she could roll out. She lifted her head up and looked at Bradley. "Good luck," she whispered.

He smiled and nodded. "You too."

She rolled out and hit the ground with a thump. "Ouch! Crap!" she whispered, as she pushed her body toward the brush on the side of the road.

Once hidden, she glanced up and saw Bradley rolling off the truck and onto the road. He rolled into the woods and out of sight. Mary was about to sigh with relief when she noticed the brake lights on the truck brighten. *Crap*, she thought, *he's stopping here.*

She was immediately on her feet and running toward him. Bradley was starting to get up when he saw her running toward her. "He's stopping," she said. "We have to get out of here now."

She grabbed his hand and they plunged together into the dense brush, running downhill from the road. A bullet hit a tree a few feet in front of them. Another hit somewhere on the ground near them. Mary pulled them to the right and they crashed through more undergrowth.

Bradley felt the burn the moment the bullet entered his foot. He kept moving, but the pain was intense. He was sure the bullet must have ricocheted off the ground first and then into his foot, because a direct shot would have caused more damage.

"We should split up," Bradley said, knowing he was going to slow them down.

"Sure," Mary panted. "You run down the hill and I'll circle back and distract him."

"Mary, no," Bradley said immediately, remembering the last thing Hank had said to him about Mary.

"Then we stick together," Mary said, turning back to look at him.

When she saw the beads of sweat on his face, she stopped. "What the hell?" she asked.

She looked down and saw the blood oozing from his boot. "You could have said something," she accused.

"There's nothing we can do right now," he said. "The boot is keeping pressure on the wound and we need to keep going."

Mary searched for a more level route to put less pressure on his foot. Cutting to the left seemed to be the most level ground of all of her choices. "Let's go this way."

They heard the engine of the truck roar to life. "Well, at least we have the advantage of being able to run through the woods," she said, pushing through the branches.

After five minutes, they found a small clearing in the midst of the woods. Mary guided Bradley to a large tree trunk. "Sit," she ordered.

He sat, wiped the sweat from his face and lifted his foot onto the log. "Mary, we need to face facts," he said. "No one knows we're out here. He has a gun, he has a truck, he has the advantage and I'm just slowing you down. We need a better plan than just trying to hide from him in the woods."

Mary shook her head. "We just need to lie low," she argued. "He won't know where to find us..."

"Mary, I've left a trail of blood across the whole damn woods," he interrupted. "Of course he can find us."

"I'm not leaving you," she said.

"Listen to me," he said. "He's not going to be half as brutal to me as he will be to you. I just can't stomach the thought of you being caught."

"But Bradley..." she began.

They heard the truck in the near distance. "Go, Mary. Go and get help," he said. "Go now!"

Mary ran across the clearing into the woods, she glanced back and saw Bradley limping away from the log and back into hiding. She really didn't want to leave him, but she knew he was right; one of them had to go and get help.

She ran southeast, toward the highway, toward help. The rough terrain was uphill and covered with a damp matting of leaves. Mary grabbed hold of branches and saplings to pull herself up toward the ridge that lay about forty feet above the maintenance road.

When she was about thirty feet up the incline she heard the truck. Looking around for cover she saw a tree trunk a few feet away lying horizontally on the ground, caught between two upright trees. She gauged the distance and jumped quickly. The move was supposed to take her sideways, toward the trunk. But her boot landed on a pile of wet leaves and her feet slipped out from under her.

She hit the ground hard and immediately began to slip downhill. Leaves, rocks and branches rolled down the hill with her. She could hear the truck's approach and knew she was on a freefall back down to the road.

Panicked, she dug her fingers into the ground, trying to grab something, anything, to hold on to. She scraped her hands on the thorny brush and jagged rocks, but couldn't find anything that would stop her descent.

Finally, she rammed into a sapling and grabbed it with both hands. She buried her face in the leaves. Praying that she was high enough on the hill and the brush was deep enough that she would be hidden. She breathed deeply, her heart pounding as she waited for the truck to pass.

The truck slowed. Mary held her breath. Then it continued down the road. Amazed and relieved, she waited a few moments before lifting her head.

The sun was beginning to set. The tree tops were ablaze in red and orange and the shadows were beginning to lengthen. Mary pulled herself up and scrambled up the rest of the incline until she reached the top of the ridge. Once there, she leaned against a big oak and caught her breath. She could hear the truck in the distance, but then the engine stopped.

Had he found Bradley? She prayed he was still safe.

"Do you love him?" a woman's voice asked.

Mary's heart jumped. She turned and found Renee Peterson next to her. The sun shone through her translucent form, giving her an ethereal glow. Her face was ice blue, her lips purple and her hair and dress were still dripping with water.

It took Mary a moment to remember her question.

"Who?" Mary asked.

"The man in the woods," Renee asked. "The one who is bleeding. Do you love him?"

Mary sighed. "He has a wife," she said simply.

Renee smiled sadly. "I understand. It's hard not to love them, but they can't be trusted."

A tear ran down her cheek. "He killed me."

Mary shook her head. "No, you don't understand. Joseph Ryerson did not kill you."

Renee looked at her suspiciously. "Why do you say that?"

"Because the man who killed you is Hank Montague."

"Hank? Hank killed me? Why?"

"Because Hank had been killing little girls. On the night of the party he was in the process of disposing of a body and you saw him."

The ghost looked at her in disbelief. "But I didn't see anything. I had no idea," she said.

Mary shrugged. "He didn't care," she said. "He was just tying up loose ends."

"Joseph didn't kill me?" she asked in wonder.

"No, he didn't," Mary replied. "He grieved for you."

Renee looked down the ridge and then back at Mary. "So, do you love him?" she asked again.

Mary smiled. "It would be easy to do," she replied.

Mike Strong appeared next to Renee. "Then why are you running away?" he asked.

Chapter Forty-two

"I'm not running, I'm going for help," Mary said, more than slightly peeved at his insinuation.

"Well, you don't have time," Mike said. "Hank has nearly caught up with the police chief."

"How do you know?" Mary asked, already moving along the top of the ridge, back toward where she left Bradley.

"Because I was there," he said.

Mary looked down. The truck was parked below her, alongside the road. She couldn't see Hank, but he was fairly close to where she and Bradley had parted.

"What the hell do I do now?" she wondered aloud.

"He left his keys in the truck," Mike said.

"Well, why didn't you say that in the first place?" Without thinking about the consequences, she ran down the incline, not bothering to hide the noise that she was making. If Hank heard her and decided to turn back, so much the better.

She jumped onto the road about ten yards from the truck. She briefly glanced around and then sprinted toward the truck. Mary was only fifteen feet from the truck, when Hank emerged from the woods next to the road. He looked up and smiled at Mary.

"I've been waiting for you," he said.

He raised the gun and aimed.

"Run!" Mike yelled at Mary, stepping between them.

Hank looked at Mike and his eyes widened. He stepped backward, away from the ghost.

"He can see me," Mike shouted and ran toward Hank. "You son-of-a-bitch, you tried to frame me!"

Hank dropped the gun and jumped in the truck. Mary could hear the ignition grind, then Hank gunned the engine and tore down the road. Mike followed, hovering over the ground and matching his speed with the truck, the rope that still hung from his neck waving in the wind.

Mary stopped at the edge of the road and watched. Hank was swerving back and forth on the road, driving at breakneck speed and Mike was right behind him. Suddenly, at the bend in the road, Renee stepped out. Her face blue and distorted, her hair and clothes dripping wet. She moved directly in front of the oncoming truck.

Hank swerved and the truck left the road. It dove into the ditch, rolled over and finally careened into a giant oak tree. A thick low-hanging branch shattered the windshield and plunged into the cab of the truck.

Moments later, Mike reappeared at Mary's side. "He's not dead," he said, "but he won't be going anywhere on his own."

"Thank you," she said. "You saved my life."

"I couldn't let him…" he began.

"I know, and you didn't," she said. "I'll make sure he gets blamed for your death, as well as the others.

"And Mike," she said, meeting his eyes. "Your secret is safe. Your legacy is safe."

Mike smiled. A tear ran down his distorted face. "Thank you."

Chapter Forty-three

Mary leaned back in her chair. Three days later and she was still stiff and sore. She needed to get an easier job.

"So, how are you feeling today?" Rosie asked, as she entered Mary's office. "Still aching?"

Mary turned her chair and nodded. "Yeah, I still can feel where my muscles are," she said, "each and every one of them."

"Good!" Rosie said with delight.

"I thought you were my friend."

"No, no, I mean wait until you see what I bought you," Rosie said as she dug into her oversized purse.

She drew out a small white jar. "This is a…" She brought it closer to her bifocals. "…a unique herbal remedy that heals the body and the soul in only twenty-four hours."

She looked up. "Imagine that, Mary," she said, "both body and soul in twenty-four hours."

"Wow! What a deal," Mary said, "Both body and soul. What more could you ask for?"

Rosie narrowed her eyes. "Are you making fun of my unique herbal remedy?" she asked.

Mary tried to hide her grin. "No, never," she said. "I mean, wow, twenty-four hours to take care of everything. Took God a whole week."

Rosie sniffed. "Well, at least you could try it," she said, handing it to Mary.

Mary nodded, opened the jar and sniffed. She coughed and quickly tightened the lid. "What is this made of? Yak poop?"

Rosie grabbed the jar. "It can't be that bad," she said, twisting the lid and holding the jar next to her nose.

"Oh, my," she said, her nose wrinkling as she screwed the lid back on quickly. "I think I'm going to demand my money back."

Mary smiled. "I think that's a very good idea."

"Maybe I could swap it for some lovely rocks that you lay on your body and they absorb your pain," she suggested.

"Or you could just get your money back," Mary said, swinging her chair back to her computer.

Rosie nodded and sighed. "You're just not any fun anymore."

Mary heard the door close and sighed. Rosie was right; she wasn't much fun right now. The head of the forensics team Bradley sent out to the fort called earlier that day. He told her they had found the remains of the girls and would be contacting their parents.

The remains of Jessica had already been found and her memorial service was scheduled for the next day. Mary hadn't decided if she was going to attend. She had met with Jessica and the other girls the day after Hank had been taken into custody. They had said their goodbyes and she knew they were already where they were supposed to be.

The families would be the ones dealing with the grief and pain.

"Which is better, hope or closure?" she wondered aloud.

"Closure," Bradley said, from the doorway.

Mary jumped at his voice, then turned and smiled.

"Good to see you on your feet, Chief," she said.

Using a wooden cane, he limped into the room, the small cast on his foot leading the way. He lowered himself into a chair. "I needed to get out of my office for a few minutes," he said, "and I wanted to make sure you heard about the girls."

She nodded. "I got the call this morning," she said. "Thanks for moving it along so quickly."

"Well, Montague was in no position to deny that he had confessed to the murders," he said. "He's still babbling about seeing ghosts."

Mary smiled. "Imagine that."

Bradley chuckled for a moment and then his face turned thoughtful. "I didn't want the families to have to wait any longer. Now they can finally move on."

Mary nodded. "I can't imagine what those families went through for all of those years," she said. "How do you go on with your life?"

Bradley sighed. "You go on because you have to," he said. "Because if you don't, you will go crazy."

"You sound like you have experience with this kind of thing," Mary said.

Bradley shrugged. "I'll tell you about it sometime," he said. "But now I have to get back to my office."

He hobbled over to the door, stopped and turned back to Mary. "Are you ever going to tell me what went on in the back of Hank's truck?" he asked. "Something tells me that it's important to remember, but my memory is still fuzzy."

Mary shook her head. "I really can't think of anything that stands out," she said evasively. "But if I do, I'll let you know."

Bradley nodded. "You do that," he said.

He grabbed the door handle, walked out of the doorway and just before he closed the door said, "By the way, Mary, my wife's name was Jeannine."

About the author:

Terri Reid lives near Freeport, the home of the Mary O'Reilly Mystery Series, and loves a good ghost story. She lives in a hundred-year-old farmhouse complete with its own ghost. She loves hearing from her readers at author@terrireid.com.

Books by Terri Reid:

Loose Ends – A Mary O'Reilly Paranormal Mystery (Book One)

Good Tidings – A Mary O'Reilly Paranormal Mystery (Book Two)

Never Forgotten – A Mary O'Reilly Paranormal Mystery (Book Three)

Final Call – A Mary O'Reilly Paranormal Mystery (Book Four)

Darkness Exposed – A Mary O'Reilly Paranormal Mystery (Book Five)

Natural Reaction – A Mary O'Reilly Paranormal Mystery (Book Six)

Secret Hollows – A Mary O'Reilly Paranormal Mystery (Book Seven)

Broken Promises – A Mary O'Reilly Paranormal Mystery (Book Eight)

Twisted Paths – A Mary O'Reilly Paranormal Mystery (Book Nine)

Veiled Passages – A Mary O'Reilly Paranormal Mystery (Book Ten)

Bumpy Roads – A Mary O'Reilly Paranormal Mystery (Book Eleven)

The Ghosts Of New Orleans – A Paranormal Research and Containment Division (PRCD) Case File